Pirate's Cove

Pirate's Cove

Brendan Clarkin

HarperCollins*Publishers (New Zealand) Limited*

To Liam, Kieran and Kate: my not-so-buried treasure.

Thanks to Sandi, Hejdi, Ann, Jim, Eunice and Room 3,
2000, for awesome advice and encouragement.
Special thanks to Tracey Wogan for sensitive, incisive
editing skills.
A big thank you to Ian, Lorain and all the crew at
HarperCollins*Publishers* for making this dream a reality.

National Library of New Zealand Cataloguing-in-Publication Data

Clarkin, Brendan, 1958-
Pirate's cove / Brendan Clarkin.
ISBN 1-86950-411-9
[1. Adventure and adventurers – Fiction.] 1. Children's stories, New Zealand.
I. Title.
NZ823.3 – dc 21

First published 2002
HarperCollins*Publishers (New Zealand) Limited*
P. O. Box 1, Auckland

ISBN 1 86950 411 9

Designed and typeset by Janine Brougham
Printed by Griffin Press, South Australia, on 50 gsm Ensobulky

Chapter 1

The darkness hanging over Pirate's Cove was almost complete. All that could be seen through the thick, black gloom was a blanket of mist hanging over the water. The water lapped quietly on the shore, the only movement to be seen in the cold hours before dawn.

Or was it the only movement?

A sharp eye might have caught a glimpse of something, a hint of movement some distance from the shore. If anyone had been watching that is. Of course no one was looking out over the water at that time of the morning. Anyone with any sense was tucked up snugly in bed, sleeping peacefully.

But if someone *had* been watching, they might just have seen the ripples. Ripples widening in the wake of . . . *something?*

Yes . . . *there!*

There was definitely something moving slowly across the surface of the water. Something black . . . shining . . . slipping silently through the water. The creature carved a smooth path, moving ever closer to the shore. Drawing near the small, sandy beach, it slowed. Raising its bulky head from the water, it seemed to sniff the air, as if trying to sense danger. The creature's head, trailing streams of water and slimy seaweed, turned slowly from right to left and back again. Searching for any movement, *any* sound.

After long silent minutes and finally sure there was no threat, the creature's jaw dropped suddenly, splashing into the water. A wet, slippery tongue emerged from its mouth and brushed over thick lips, wetting the rubbery surface.

Out of the water, the creature's breath rasped, the only sound to be heard in the stillness of the night. The snake-like eyes flickered towards the shapes set back some distance from the shore. Shapes of buildings . . . cabins. Cabins containing people. The people were the danger the creature watched for. The threat the creature feared. The people did not know about the creature.

Yet!

Chapter 2

I could hear my mother's voice screeching at me above the sound of the cake mixer.

'*Brett Rigby!* Are you listening to me? Are you sure you've got everything packed? Have you got your tooth-brush? What about your socks . . . oh, and a towel? Now you make sure you have a shower every day, won't you? *And don't forget to change your underwear.*'

Ah . . . parents! I've said it before and I'll say it again. *They are not human.* They are designed to make life difficult for us, to drive us nuts. And boy, do my parents succeed. In fact, they nearly stopped me from going to school camp. Can you believe it?

I had been looking forward to camp for months. Talked about it. Dreamed about it. Spent *hours* thinking about it. Finally, there I was, all packed and ready to go. Just sitting at the dining table, waiting for Dad to drop me off at school to catch the bus.

It was only six o'clock and the bus wasn't due to leave until seven that evening. Plenty of time, but no way was I going to be late. Not for school camp. So I sat. And waited. Time to kill and nothing good on TV. And then Amanda, my baby sister, walked into the dining room and started winding me up.

'Oh Lean Bean, guess what I'm going to do while you're at camp?'

My nickname at home is 'Lean Bean' because I'm so skinny. Skinny and short. I'm shorter than other kids my age and I also don't have much hair on account of a bet I lost at school. The winner got to give me a free haircut at lunchtime. Add to that a bad dose of freckles and I don't make a pretty picture. After the 'free haircut', it was only three days before Mum started talking to me again.

Amanda hassles me all the time about my hair, my freckles . . . anything! So this was nothing new. Of course, I ignored her. That's what you do with little sisters. Actually she's only a year younger and she's nearly as tall as me, but I call her my baby sister just to annoy her. Works too.

Unfortunately, at that moment, it was Amanda who was annoying me. 'I'm going to go into your room and get into *all* your things.'

I pushed myself up off the chair and stomped into the lounge, struggling to keep a grip on my temper. Camp was too close to let her spoil my day. Amanda followed, fluffing up her blonde, curly hair like a peacock preening its feathers. Like me, she's skinny, but in looks she takes more after Mum. All I got from Dad was freckles and a sticky-up nose.

Amanda whispered. She cooed like a dove in that sickly 'little girl' voice she saves just for me. The voice you can't hear in the next room. You know, the room where the parents are. Oh no, they *never* hear the things she says to wind me up. They *never* see the things she does that cause me to lose my temper. All they ever hear and see is mean big brother Brett picking on dear little sister Amanda.

Amanda continued whining. 'You've got lots of interesting things in your room. Things you think I don't know about. Wouldn't want Mum and Dad to find out, would we?'

I started to spin out. I could feel the heat rising through my body, my face going red.

'I'm going into your wardrobe, I know what you keep in there. On the top shelf at the back. You know what I'm talking about, don't you?'

That was when I cracked. Lost the plot. Spat the dummy. You name it, I did it. Big time! I didn't touch her. Oh no. I learned early on that getting rough with Amanda only made Mum and Dad even madder at me. But I did go absolutely nuts. Called her a few choice names even she hadn't heard before.

Let her pet mouse Wilbur out of its cage. Oh, and let the cat into the room at the same time. I think that was what really did it. Yes, until the cat arrived, Amanda was just coping. Looking pale, yes, after copping a mouthful from me. Looking hassled, definitely, with her mouse hightailing it under the couch. But the cat, that sent her truly ballistic.

'*Aaaaagh!* Mum . . . Dad . . . Brett's killing Wilbur. Save him! *Aaaaaaaaagh!*'

For that brief moment, listening to her scream as if her life was about to end, it almost made being her brother worthwhile. Briefly, that is, until my parents arrived on the scene.

'What's going on in here? What are you two doing *now?*' This was Mum, wailing and waving a wooden spoon dripping cake mixture.

'Dammit. *What now?* Why can't you kids *ever* do anything without ending up fighting?' This was Dad, shouting at the top of his voice, face red, fit to bust.

'Brett's set the cat on Wilbur. *He's killing him!*'

'*Sheee* started it. She's bugging me like she always does.'

And on and on it went. Wilbur somewhere under the couch, no doubt messing himself in absolute terror. The cat stalking around the couch, pawing at one side and then the other in the hope of a free lunch. Amanda screaming, jumping up and down and doing nothing useful to save her precious Wilbur. Me backed in the corner knowing I was in deep trouble. Mum shaking the wooden spoon at me, telling me how horrible I was. Dad swearing and chasing after the cat, trying to shoo it out of the room.

I stood there speechless. Couldn't think of anything to say that would help me. Boy was that something! Normally I have the opposite problem. I talk too much. Mum reckons I talk so much because I'm small for my age. I have to work to get attention. At least that's what she says.

I guess there's something to it. All the other guys my age are a good head taller than me. I can't compete with them in the physical stuff, so I have to get the best of them with my mouth. It works most of the time, although I've been in a few fights from giving too much lip. *And* a few detentions. I can't help myself sometimes. The words come out my mouth before the thoughts are sorted in my head.

Anyway, when things finally calmed down, Mum and Dad threatened to send me to the basement for the week . . . *no camp!* I went hot and cold all over. They knew how much I had been looking forward to camp. Boy, parents sure know how to play dirty and use things against you.

In the end, I think the only reason I got to go to camp was so they could get rid of me for a week and have some peace and quiet. *Parents!*

Chapter 3

Three hours later, the bus arrived at camp. I actually sighed, I was so happy. One whole week on school camp with no annoying sister and no nagging parents.

Paradise!

Pirate's Cove had to be the most awesome camp out. I had never been there, but the older kids at my school — Allenvale School — said it was totally cool. Even the name was wicked: Pirate's Cove . . . *yeah!*

We piled off the bus, all thirty of us chattering and laughing, pushing and shoving, ready for a week of pure fun. There were bodies, bags and pillows flying in all directions.

There was also Mr McArthur, our teacher, a bunch of parent helpers and three senior kids who were on camp the previous year. They were there to help as activity leaders. After a brief meeting in the dining hall to have supper and sort out where we were sleeping, we were shunted off to our cabins to settle in for the night. *Yeah right!*

Let's do the maths here. Six eleven-year-old boys plus first night of camp plus sleeping in a cabin equals fun, big time and practical jokes. *Right?*

Right! But you have to be patient. Start too early and

you have teachers and parents breathing down your neck. So we waited.

The cabins were old and cramped, almost like cells in a jail. Small windows up high on the walls let in the only light from outside but they were so high you couldn't see out.

Three sets of bunks were jammed up against each other along one wall. The only place to store gear was on the floor under the bottom bunks. The floor was bare concrete with just a small carpet square to remind you that this wasn't actually a prison cell. Home, sweet home, for a whole week. Not exactly luxury, but hey, this was camp and nothing beat camp! According to the older kids it was the best part of the year.

So there we were in our sleeping bags, 'settling in' for the first night of school camp. 'Settling in' means being quiet enough to keep the teachers and parents on guard happy. They liked to patrol up and down outside our cabins for an hour or so until they were sure we were asleep.

'So what's the deal with Pirate's Cove?' I whispered. 'Anyone know how the camp got its name?'

'I do,' popped up a squeaky voice, eager to please.

We all groaned. *Kenneth*. It had to be Kenneth Thompson.

Steve Simmons threw his pillow at Kenneth's head. 'Pipe down, Brain Drain. You're only here because we didn't have a choice of roommates.'

Silence.

'Well, doesn't *anyone else* know how it got its name?' I pleaded.

More silence.

I groaned to myself. 'All right Kenneth, let's hear it. But keep it brief and try to talk in a language we can understand.'

Kenneth is living proof that aliens walk among us. We came to this conclusion long ago. Not only does he know too much, he knows things kids should simply not know. He discusses politics, religion and economics — whatever that is — with Mr McArthur. I rest my case.

The aliens really stuffed up when they programmed Kenneth before sending him to earth. For a start, they could have packaged him better. It doesn't help that he's even shorter than me, has short spiky hair, wears glasses and is shaped like a box. He actually appears to be as wide as he is tall. I know he can't help that, but hey, you know what boys are like. You always have to have someone to pick on, and in our class, Kenneth was the one.

And then they put an adult's brain in a boy's body. You see, Kenneth knows *everything!* Doesn't matter what question the teacher asks, Kenneth always knows the answer. Sometimes he even answers questions *before* Mr McArthur has finished asking them. Now, how bad is that?

We waited nervously for Kenneth to start, certain we were going to be bored with another one of his dull lectures. For once, Kenneth surprised us.

'Did you guys know this camp is haunted?'

Chapter 4

Pirate's Cove Camp is in a regional park on a point sticking out into the sea, Kenneth tells us. To the left of the point is a huge cove, almost like a lake.

'Apparently, a couple of hundred years ago, a pirate ship called the *Revenge* arrived in the cove. It was being chased by privateers and sailed into the cove under cover of darkness to avoid being captured. The pirate captain — his name was Jonah Bailey — hoped the privateers chasing him would sail past the cove and down the coast.'

'Hold on, Egghead,' Steve grumbled, 'you've lost me already. I know what pirates are, but what the heck are privateers?'

Even I knew the answer to that one. I spoke up quickly before Kenneth had a chance to reply. 'Sort of like bounty hunters. The government gave them permission to attack pirates and ships from other countries. Right, Kenneth?'

'Yes. That's right.'

Now, I'm not the smartest kid on the block, so I lay there feeling very satisfied at proving I'm not a total dummy.

Kenneth continued his story. 'Anyway, nobody knows

for sure what happened. Some say the privateers spotted the *Revenge* in the cove and blocked the entrance. Then they anchored some distance from the pirates and blew them out of the water with their cannon.'

'Cool.'

'Awesome.'

We were all impressed. A little blood and guts goes a long way.

'Others say the privateers did sail past the cove and down the coast. Uncertain if it was safe to sail the *Revenge* back out to sea, Captain Bailey sank it close to the shore in the cove and marked the spot so he could return when it was safe to recover his treasure. They say he slaughtered all of his crew so no one could reveal the *Revenge*'s hiding place.'

'Freaky.'

'That's gross, man.'

'Yeah, cool eh?'

Kenneth carried on, encouraged by having impressed us. 'Nobody knows for sure what really happened, but people say the ghosts of the murdered pirates haunt the cove. They say they come up on land at night to see if the way is clear for them to escape. That's how it came to be called Pirate's Cove.'

I snuggled down a little deeper in my sleeping bag. Thinking about the ghosts of dead pirates walking around camp at night was not a nice thought. I was annoyed that Kenneth had scared me with his ghost story. Still, he would keep. I had something in store for him.

Chapter 5

O K, OK, don't freak.

Before you go all sad on me, he didn't eat any. He did come close . . . but not quite. *Of course I wouldn't have let him eat them!* I'm not that gross.

The fun is in watching someone spin out, not actually making them sick. And boy did Kenneth spin out. I knew what was coming of course, so I watched his face carefully as I passed him the packet. 'Here, have some of these.'

A huge grin on his face, Kenneth said, 'Cool, thanks.'

He was so grateful, I almost felt sorry for him. He stuck his chubby fingers in the packet and pulled out a handful of the 'raisins'. Trouble was, the 'raisins' weren't quite what he was expecting. Not smooth, hard, dark chocolate. Instead, soft, crumbling, sticky rabbit poo. Oh, and just starting to go really smelly.

You keep them for a few days in the hot-water cupboard to get them like that. Don't forget to add a little water to keep them soggy. Can't have them drying out.

Kenneth did not disappoint. The look on his face went from:

1. surprise that I would share my sweets with him, to;

2. delight at an unexpected pig-out, to;
3. puzzlement when the 'raisins' did not feel or look like they should, to;
4. total horror when he clicked what he was actually holding.

And that was when he screamed.

Yes, he *actually* screamed! Or squealed would be a better description of the gross noise that came out of his mouth. Whatever, it was loud and long.

'*Aaaaaaaaaaargh*. What is it? Oooooh, that's so foul. It stinks! Are you trying to kill me?'

Of course, I'd let the other guys know what was coming. And boy did we bust our guts laughing. Real tears-in-the-eyes stuff! My stomach hurt for hours afterward. Oh, but the pain was worth it. And so was Mr McArthur's reaction when he burst in through the door.

Mr McArthur is OK as far as teachers go, I guess. He can be pretty cool, but he also has a grumpy side — usually when I wind him up, which is fairly regularly. Macca (that's what we call him, though not to his face of course) still has most of his hair and is tall and skinny. Makes him look a bit like a grasshopper, especially when he's leaning over a desk. In class, he wears these glasses that he only needs for reading. You know, the ones that have the top half cut off. He's always staring over the top of them at us and though he's not that old, the glasses don't help. They make him look like an old man out of a kid's picture book.

Anyway, like I said, he's OK as a teacher and he sees

the funny side of things occasionally. Not that night, however.

About thirty seconds after Kenneth started wailing, the cabin door burst open with a crash. Mr McArthur stood in the doorway, eyes all red, his jaw flapping. 'What . . . what on earth is going on in here? *Who is making that awful noise?*'

He was fuming; spitting mad. Normally that would have been enough to shut us all up. He can be really scary when he wants to be. There was just one problem this time. You see, Macca was standing there in his boxers. Yes, in his boxers. *How gross!* And that sent us into another round of gut-busting laughter.

Mr McArthur, standing there shaking with fury and wearing boxers covered in cuddly teddy bears with the words 'I can't bear to be without you!' written across them. I didn't even want to think about who gave them to him. Even when Macca roared at me, I wasn't too bothered.

'*Brett Rigby, you're the cause of this, aren't you?*'

I was still laughing so much I couldn't even talk. I just nodded my head, tears streaming from my eyes.

'Right,' Macca bellowed again. 'You're out of here. *Now!*'

That sobered me up pretty quickly. 'What . . . what's happening? Where am I going, sir?'

'Outside. You can't sleep in here without causing problems, so you can get a bit of fresh air for the night. See how you like that!'

'But . . .'

'No buts, Rigby. Get your sleeping bag and move. You're outside on the concrete. *For the whole night.*'

Unbelievable! First night of camp and I was in major trouble. It just wasn't fair! It was only some innocent fun; the one thing I am really good at. Sadly, it's a talent some people don't seem to appreciate. By 'people', you know who I mean.

Parents . . . teachers . . . I guess you could say adults in general. It puzzles me sometimes — I do something funny, not really *that* bad, and what happens? Kids laugh and adults spew.

So, I ended up shivering in my sleeping bag on the cold, concrete path outside the cabin. And I wasn't even allowed to take my pillow. Not that I was thinking about complaining. I was too busy trying to get comfortable and stay warm.

And the cold wasn't the only thing making me shiver. It was the thought of ghosts! And I guess that's how Kenneth got his revenge. Now, I don't believe in ghosts, but there I was, stranded outside all alone, with absolutely nothing between me and the cove at the bottom of the slope.

From where I was lying I could have thrown a stone into the dark, gloomy water of the cove. *It was that close!* It did not make me feel happy.

I could have killed Kenneth! This ghost story was typical of him. It wasn't just what he said; it was the fact that *he* told the story. Anyone else, we would have laughed it off. But like I said, Kenneth knows everything. He gets everything right! So if he says the bay is haunted and there are ghosts, then there are.

Hey . . . what was that?

Chapter 6

I was asleep and dreaming. Having a nightmare actually. In the nightmare I was tied up so tight I couldn't move, and two pale white hands with long skinny fingers were closing around my neck. Squeezing.

Except . . . it wasn't a nightmare.

It was real!

I lashed out against the ghostly hands trying to strangle me, but I couldn't get my hands free. They were stuck inside my sleeping bag. That didn't stop me screaming though. '*Aaargh* . . . get away . . . get off me! *Heeelp!*'

The hands dropped off my neck. 'Settle down, you idiot. No need to go hyper. Macca said to come and wake you up. It's breakfast time.'

Heart pounding in my chest and squinting painfully against the early morning sunlight, I made out the disgusted face of Danny Martin.

Relieved and embarrassed, I collapsed back onto the concrete. Danny is one of my best friends. His thin, black hair slicked back, he looked like he'd just stepped out of the shower. He certainly looked a lot fresher than I felt. Although he's taller and stronger than me, Danny is definitely not as smart.

'What's the matter?' Danny asked, puzzled. 'Didn't you sleep well?'

'What do you think?' I spat back. 'Why don't you try spending the night on a hard concrete path being woken every five minutes by . . . by . . . noises and . . . the cold. See how happy you'd be in the morning.'

No way was I going to admit to Danny or anyone else that fear of ghosts had kept me wide awake most of the night.

He pulled a face. 'Yeah, I suppose you're right. Mind you, it was worth it. You got Kenneth a beauty and then to have Macca walk in like that . . . *awesome!* That's all anyone is talking about this morning.'

I managed a weak grin in spite of my tiredness. 'Cool. And how is Macca this morning?'

'Fine, I guess. He hasn't said a word about last night. Though . . .' Danny's voice trailed away weakly.

The grin dropped from my face. 'Though what?'

'Well, he hasn't *said* anything, but he certainly hasn't forgotten what you did.'

Confused and worried, I sat up in my bag. 'What do you mean? What's he done?'

'He's posted the groups for our camp activities on the notice board in the dining room.'

'So?'

'So . . . he's teamed you with Kenneth Thompson and Emily Burton.'

I groaned and pulled the sleeping bag over my head. Macca had truly taken his revenge in the worst possible way. Any other punishment would have been fine. Doing lines, washing dishes, picking up rubbish . . . even cleaning toilets would have been better than this.

But Macca knew that. He had gone straight for the throat and saddled me for the entire camp with the two biggest losers in the class. Kenneth you know about. Enough said about him.

As for Emily Burton . . . words almost fail me. Not because I don't know what to say, I just don't know where to start. Life for Emily is a breeze. She is good at sport and always in the top teams. And talk about smart! She thinks any mark under ninety per cent is a failure.

Emily is a trendy girl; brown hair cut short, always dressed in the latest fashions. She is tall and not bad-looking actually. Until she opens her mouth. Spoils it every time. You see, Emily is so nice she makes me want to puke. A real Miss Goody-Two-Shoes. Always poking her nose into other people's business. If anyone is in trouble, who's the one always there to help them out? You guessed it . . . Emily Burton! Always standing up for someone, whether they want help or not. And worst of all, she has enough conscience to make up for the rest of us who like to push it aside from time to time.

If you want to cause trouble, even if it is just a little innocent fun, make sure Emily is at least two blocks away. She can smell trouble coming and sees it as her duty in life to fight the forces of evil. No one, but no one, has dobbed me in more times than Emily.

Oh, this was undoubtedly the worst! Macca must have

been *really* steamed to do this to me. Sentenced me to five days with (1) a watchdog who wouldn't even let me breathe at the wrong time without letting me know about it, and (2) a space cadet from somewhere past Venus who is just loopy enough to actually frighten me.

Chapter 7

'It's over *here*. I'm sure it is. *Aaaagh* . . . watch out! They're everywhere, all around us. Take that . . . *and that!*'

This was Kenneth, alias Darth Doorknob, slashing violently through shrubs and flax with a hockey stick, trying to find an orienteering marker. From the way he swung the stick, it was obvious he was holding a light-saber, fighting off the hordes of Zarbeelian mud monsters surrounding him.

Obvious to no one but Kenneth, that is. After less than two hours I was already beginning to understand what was going through his mind. It was truly frightening!

'Kenneth, I really don't think you should be using the stick like that. You might damage those plants. Some of them are still quite young and tender.'

This was Sister Mary Emily doing what she does best; playing at being mother . . . teacher . . . policewoman.

Though we were in the same team, I tried to stay away from the two of them as much as possible. I was terrified some of Emily's sickly sweet goodness might rub off on me. And I was dead scared I might catch some of Kenneth's loopiness.

I stood still and shook my head. I was still in shock,

hours after being landed with . . . *them!* Frustration finally got the best of me.

'Aw, come on you guys. We've been out here for over an hour trying to find this last marker. Get a grip, Kenneth. And Emily, would you shut up and stop your whining? All the other teams finished ages ago. They're probably inside pigging out on biscuits and cake while we're wasting time wandering round in the wilderness trying to find a stupid piece of painted tin.'

Emily gave me her stern look. 'Now, don't be so negative, Brett. If you had a better attitude you would enjoy yourself and get more out of this.'

If anyone starts telling me what to do, especially when I'm unhappy, they get a lethal response quicker than you can strike a match. But Emily . . . she is just *sooo* unreal. I spluttered, like a lawnmower that wouldn't start. I couldn't think of *anything* to say to her.

Finally, I shook my head in disgust and waved my hand towards Kenneth. 'Just . . . just go and get the idiot boy and we'll look closer to the water again. Down there by that shed. I'm *sure* the marker is there somewhere.'

I stomped off grumpily, without waiting for a reply. Only the first full day of camp — the camp I had been so looking forward to — and already I was longing to go home!

We had been searching the bush near the edge of the cove for the very last marker. According to the map, it was located at the bottom of the slope near a small shed. Our first look around the shed turned up nothing. I moved in closer to the shed once more. Searching the area of bush just behind it, I found . . . nothing. Again!

Frustrated and bored witless, I walked over and peered through the dusty, cobwebbed window at the back of the shed. I could see the outline of a door on the opposite wall.

An untidy pile of garden tools was stacked messily in the corner to the right of the door. To the left, a bench was cluttered with small tools, tins and cans. The walls were covered with hooks from which all sorts of junk was hanging. Just beneath the window lay a messy heap of sacks and wooden crates.

And right beside the window, turning towards me and glaring, was the ugliest face I had ever seen!

Chapter 8

Not only was the man ugly, he was steaming as well. He yelled at me through the glass.

'What are ya pokin' your nose in here for? Go on, clear off! This is private property.'

'Uh . . . sorry, mister,' I stuttered. 'I . . . I thought it was part of the camp.'

The door slammed, and the man strode around the corner of the shed to meet me. Kenneth and Emily arrived puffing, drawn by the yelling.

'It *is* part of the camp,' the man continued, eyeing us up and down, 'but it's out of bounds to campers. I'm the caretaker here and all my stuff is stored in the shed. Dangerous stuff as well,' he added, his lips parting in a wicked grin.

The three of us stood there like dummies. Staring. Not saying anything. All thinking the same thing. *What ugly, evil black teeth he's got!*

Surely this is what pirates must have looked like all those years ago? He looked pretty old too, maybe in his forties. Black whiskers covered his face with dark, greasy hair dangling over his eyes. His face was thin, the bones sticking out like a skeleton and his nose was bent badly to one side. This man had seen a few fights.

'So kiddies,' he continued, still grinning, 'how's the camp going?'

The shock of his sudden and unpleasant appearance was beginning to wear off. Being called a 'kiddy' also helped get me back to my normal self.

'Not bad, *Pop*,' I replied cheekily. 'How's your day going?'

The evil grin disappeared from his face and his eyes narrowed as he glared straight at me. 'Good, until you poked your nose in where it wasn't wanted, *sonny*. You really don't want to do that again. Unpleasant things can happen.'

I swallowed hard, not so sure of myself. My mind was racing, but before I could think of a smart reply, Emily spoke up all sweet and innocent.

'What do you mean? Surely it's safe here? They wouldn't let us come here if it was dangerous. *Would they?*'

'Oh no, Missy. It's safe. Just as long as you play where you should . . . and mind your own business.'

He shifted his gaze from Emily back to me as he spoke these last words, his message loud and clear. Clear at least to me, but Little Miss Innocent kept on burbling as if we had just made a new friend. 'Well, that's fine then. We're all here to have a good time, certainly not to cause any bother. So it won't be a problem.'

The man shifted closer to me, reached out one grubby hand and patted me on the shoulder. He was a little too rough for my liking. 'Well that's just dandy then. We'll all get along fine. My name's Watson. But everybody calls me Watty. What do you call yourselves?'

Something in my guts didn't want him to know who I was. But before I could say anything, Kenneth blundered into the conversation. 'I'm Kenneth, she's Emily and he's Brett. We're all in the same room at school.'

Watty grinned, showing us those revolting teeth once more. 'Well, isn't that nice.'

He reached out and shook our hands. Mine ached after he let go. All I wanted to do was get away from this man, but Kenneth spoke again. 'If you work here, you must know some of the history of this place.'

Watty's eyes shone wickedly as he cackled in response to Kenneth's question. 'I know what you're getting at. You want to know about the pirates . . . and the ghosts. Right?'

Kenneth's eyes widened. 'You know about the stories, then?'

'Sure do. And you know what?' Watty leaned in so close we could smell him. He stank of diesel and sweat. His voice dropped so low he was almost whispering. *The stories are true!*'

There was a long silence as his words sunk in. Finally I managed to find my voice. It was a little squeaky, not nearly as brave as I wanted it to sound. 'Nah, there's no such thing as ghosts. That's a load of old rubbish.'

Watty straightened up, his eyes boring into me. I felt like he could see right through me. 'Think so, do you? Well, maybe you're right. But folks say things happen around here at night that can't be explained. I'm not sure what I believe, but I'd suggest you all stay tucked up safe and sound in your beds. It's the best place for you if you want to stay healthy.'

I said nothing, convinced this was just another warning from Watty to watch myself. Kenneth, fool that he is, said 'wow' and 'wicked', thinking this was all a great game.

Emily, for the first time, actually said something that pleased me. 'Well, I don't believe in ghosts. And I don't think you should frighten us by going on about them. It's not nice.'

To my surprise, Watty actually backed off and threw up his hands. 'Hey, I'm sorry if I scared you.' He pointed at Kenneth. 'I was just answering your friend's question.' He looked at me once more, his eyes narrowing. 'And I really don't want to see *anyone* get hurt. That's all.'

Mother Emily took control of the situation. 'Well, it's been nice to meet you, but I think we'd better get back. We've been away long enough. Goodbye.'

She turned and started walking back up the slope to the main camp buildings. Kenneth cheerfully waved goodbye and trotted obediently after Emily.

I didn't wave and I didn't say goodbye. I just followed after them. When I got to the top of the slope, I turned and looked back. Watty hadn't moved. He was still standing there by the shed. Watching.

I shivered, and ran to catch up with Kenneth and Emily.

What was wrong with them? Was I the only one who could see that there was something funny about Watty? I didn't trust him one little bit.

When we got back to the dining room and were sitting with our drinks and cake, I talked to them about it. 'Boy, is that guy Watty a nutcase or what?'

Emily looked puzzled. 'What do you mean, Brett? He wasn't very clean and he did smell a bit. But that doesn't make him a nutcase, whatever that is.'

'Oh, come on,' I pleaded, 'couldn't you see it? There's definitely something not right about him.'

Kenneth shrugged his shoulders. 'He looked OK to me, and he knows stuff about the pirates and ghosts. I wanted to hear more.'

I groaned out loud. 'Didn't you see the way he looked at me? And what about when he shook hands? He almost crushed mine. And . . . and he smells and he's dirty and . . . and what about those teeth?'

Emily shook her finger at me sternly. 'That's not fair, Brett. After all, he is the caretaker. You have to expect him to be dirty. And as for his teeth, well, they weren't very nice, but you can't judge a book by its cover.'

'Yeah, yeah, I know all that. But there's something about him that's not right. I don't trust him.'

Now it was Kenneth's turn to lecture me. Being around Emily was not doing him any good. 'Takes one to know one, I guess, Brett. After what you did to me last night in the cabin, I sure don't trust you.'

I gave up. Threw my hands in the air and walked away

from the two of them. I didn't know why I was bothering talking to them. After all, activities were over for the day and I didn't even have to *be* with them anymore.

Chapter 9

That night, I lay in bed wide awake. I should have been asleep after a busy day and not much sleep the night before. But no!

I lay there listening to Kenneth snore and Danny talk in his sleep. My mind was racing and wouldn't slow down, thinking about how camp was not turning out the way I had hoped. Thinking about pirates and ghosts. And thinking about Watty.

So I lay there, wide awake, trying to figure it all out. Especially why I didn't trust Watty.

Some time after midnight I gave up thinking. It hurt too much. And I needed to go to the toilet. I slipped out of my sleeping bag and pulled on a sweatshirt to go over to the boys' toilet block. It was next to the main camp building.

Quietly opening the door, I took a quick look down towards the cove. Just to make sure there was nothing . . .

Aaaaghhhh, stupid Kenneth and his stupid ghost stories. They had totally freaked me out. Mind you, Watty didn't help by going on the way he did. Peering down towards the cove, I couldn't see any ghosts, not that I knew what ghosts looked like.

But . . . there was something moving down at the water's edge.

And I was sure I could hear voices. Muffled whispers among the trees just past Watty's shed.

I walked a little further down the slope to get a better view, then stopped dead in my tracks. *What was I doing?*

I must have been out of my mind! It was the middle of the night in a strange place with strange people and I was going exploring. Alone. *How smart was that?* Not very! And that's when I noticed that the noises and movement down by the cove had also stopped.

That was enough for me. I turned and ran back to the cabin as fast as I could for help.

Kenneth was not my first choice to take on a midnight adventure, but he was the one who had started all of this. He was the one who wanted to find out about ghosts, so I woke him instead of Danny. It took ages to stir him and get him out of bed. As he fumbled around pulling on clothes by the light of a torch, I explained what I had seen and heard.

Now as we walked down the slope in the darkness, Kenneth in front and me behind, I kept poking him. He was so slow and awkward. '*Owww!* Stop pushing me.'

'Hurry up, Kenneth,' I grumbled. 'And stop making so much noise. They'll hear us with you bumbling along like this.'

'Who will hear us?' Kenneth whined, still half asleep. He was not a happy boy.

'I don't know,' I snapped. 'That's why you're here. To help me find out. Now keep moving and shut up.'

After what seemed like hours, but was probably only a few minutes, we made it to the bottom of the slope. Straight ahead was the small sandy beach. Some distance away to our left was the caretaker's shed. We could barely make it out in the dim moonlight. To our right was the boatshed where all the kayaks were stored.

'So what do we do now?' Kenneth whispered nervously. 'Look, there's nothing here. Can I please go back to bed? *Please?*'

'No! And stop your moaning.'

Impatiently, I brushed past Kenneth and stared into the trees by the shed, where I had seen the movement.

Nothing. It was hopeless!

With the moon behind the clouds, it was too dark to make anything out. And if anyone had been there, the noise we had made coming down the hill would surely have frightened them off.

I could feel my heart thumping in my chest and my mouth was dry. But I kept moving towards the trees. I had seen and heard something and I was going to find out what it was.

I stopped to pick up a stick from the ground. I didn't know what I would do with it, but no way was I going into the trees without some protection. After all, Kenneth didn't count for much.

Entering the first stand of trees, I paused. It was even darker in here than out in the open. Still, nothing moved.

I walked further into the bush, heart racing, hands sweaty on the branch. And then stopped dead in my tracks when I heard a noise.

A noise coming from behind me, *not in front!* Like twigs breaking under someone's foot. I might as well have brought a herd of African elephants with me.

'Dammit, Kenneth,' I whispered nervously over my shoulder, 'can't you do *anything* right? Walk quietly. *Lift your feet*, you great clod.'

Kenneth did not reply.

'Ken . . . Kenneth! Are you there?'

No answer. No sound. Nothing at all.

My own breathing now sounded so loud, I was sure anyone standing nearby would be able to hear it. And then I heard the noise again. Still behind me, but closer now.

I couldn't move. My feet were frozen in place and I could feel my heart pounding in my chest. And I couldn't turn around to see where Kenneth was. What if he wasn't there? What if someone or *something* else was there?

Again the noise. Like leaves being crunched by something heavy. Much heavier than Kenneth. It was right behind me now!

'Kenneth,' I wailed, now totally freaked out. I could feel a trail of cold sweat trickling down my back. '*Kenneth!* Is that you? *Kenneth, where are you?*'

Finally I knew it wasn't Kenneth behind me. *It couldn't be Kenneth!* He was smaller than me and the thing behind me was breathing right down my neck. *I could feel and smell its rotting breath!*

Total panic finally gave my legs the energy they needed to move. To run . . . to escape.

But it was too late.

As I took my first panicked step, quick as a flash, something foul-smelling and hairy wrapped itself around my neck and lifted me off the ground.

Chapter 10

Even though I was being strangled, I still managed a muffled scream. I thrashed about with the stick and kicked with both my feet at whatever was holding me from behind.

A deep grunt and a groan told me I was actually hurting the thing attacking me. Encouraged, I lashed out even harder and the grip on my throat loosened. Whatever was around my throat slipped up around my face.

I didn't even think about it. I just bit! Sank my teeth into gross, hairy flesh and bit and ripped as hard as I could.

An awful scream pounded my ears. A ghastly, ghostly wail like something long dead. The grip on my head loosened and I fell heavily to the ground. Panting for breath, I rolled on to my back and scrambled away on all fours like a crab, desperate to escape the clutches of the beast.

Branches and twigs scratched my face but I didn't care. I just had to get away. I scrambled and rolled frantically through the undergrowth, until my head banged painfully against something solid. Shaking my head, I looked up.

Through the dizziness and the darkness, I could just

make out the outline of something big and square. The caretaker's shed!

I crawled quickly around the corner of the shed and lay gasping for breath. After what seemed like forever, I dug up my last shred of courage and peered around the corner to see what my attacker was doing.

Through the gloom and the tears in my eyes, I could just see the creature. It was some distance away, hunched over against a tree. It groaned horribly as it held on to the limb I had ripped into with my teeth.

I could still taste sweat and blood in my mouth. I spat on the ground and my stomach heaved, ready to throw up.

Slumped over against the tree and groaning in pain, the creature looked twisted and ugly. Totally inhuman!

And then for the first time that night, the moon broke through the cloud cover and shone down brightly. I pulled back against the shed, terrified the beast would see me in the moonlight.

Chest heaving, I finally looked around again. As if sensing my presence, the creature straightened up from the tree and glared straight at me.

Its lips parted in an awful snarl, revealing rows of sharp, pointed teeth. Blackened teeth. As it straightened and snarled, I recognised the creature spotlighted by the moon.

It was Watty!

Chapter 11

For the second night in a row, I woke Mr McArthur up in the middle of the night. Actually it was Watty who woke him up, holding me with one hand and banging heavily on Macca's door with the other.

If anything, Macca looked worse than he did the previous night. His hair was all over the place and his eyes were all red. The only good thing was he was wearing track pants when he answered the door, and not boxers.

'Sorry to disturb you at this late hour, Mr McArthur, but I caught one of your lads down by the water. It's not the safest of places to be, so I thought you should know about it.'

'Right . . . yes . . . uh, quite right,' Macca mumbled sleepily, running a hand through his hair. Then taking a good look at me, he groaned. 'I might have known. What on earth do you think you were doing, Rigby?'

'I . . . I was . . . I saw some . . . something down by the cove.' I knew it sounded ridiculous but what else could I say. That I was searching for ghosts and pirates? Yeah right!

Watty was still holding my arm. I pulled free and pointed at him angrily. 'And then he attacked me. Tried to strangle me.'

Watty laughed. A short evil chuckle. He reached out and ruffled my hair like we were the best of pals.

'All a misunderstanding. There I was, doing my late rounds, making sure the camp was all locked up and safe, and I see someone sneaking around in the bush down by the cove. I mean, what was I supposed to think? I thought you were an intruder.'

Macca glared at me. 'Sounds reasonable to me, Rigby. You've only got yourself to blame. What a stupid thing to do. You could have gotten badly hurt.'

Watty grunted and showed Macca a ragged wound on his arm. It was still seeping blood and was already bruising around the edges. 'Talk about hurt. I think *I'm* the one who's come off worst. This is going to need a bit of treatment. Probably some stitches.'

Macca was horrified. 'That's terrible! How did that happen?'

Watty said nothing. Just looked at me, that same revolting smile on his ugly face.

I shuffled my feet nervously, feeling sicker by the minute. I simply couldn't believe it! Watty had tried to strangle me and I was the one being made to look like a criminal.

'I . . . I bit him,' I said in a quiet voice, looking down at my feet. I wished the ground would open up and swallow me. Then I looked up at Macca, pleading, 'But, but sir, he was strangling me. *I had to do something!*'

Furious now, Macca waved his hand at me. 'Enough, Rigby. I've heard all I want to hear for tonight. Get back to your cabin and stay there. I'll deal with you in the morning.'

Turning back to Watty, Macca took him gently by his good arm. 'I am so sorry about this. The boy is nothing but trouble. Come with me and I'll get this cleaned up.'

As they turned the corner to go to the sickbay, with Macca still prattling on about how sorry he was, Watty looked back over his shoulder and smirked at me.

Chapter 12

Kenneth managed to avoid me until after breakfast the next morning. I finally cornered him coming out of the dining room. 'So what happened to you last night?' I barked angrily.

He was shaking, he was so upset. 'I . . . I got lost . . . in the bush.'

'*Got lost!* Even in the dark you couldn't get lost in that bush. My grandmother couldn't get lost in there. And she's half blind. You ran away, didn't you? *Ran away and left me.*'

Angrily, he nodded. 'All right! I admit it, I ran away. There, are you satisfied? I was scared. It was dark and when I saw Watty in the bushes, I hid and then ran away.'

I was stunned. '*You saw Watty!* And you didn't warn me?'

Kenneth pleaded with me. 'How could I warn you? You were too far away, and if I'd yelled, I would have been caught as well.'

I shook my head, totally disgusted with him. Angry and disgusted. I was more angry with Watty than Kenneth, but I couldn't take it out on Watty, so I gave Kenneth an earful instead.

I told him exactly what had happened. I made special

mention of Watty trying to strangle me, just to make him feel bad. When I finished, he said . . . nothing. Just stood there, head hanging down.

Then, joy of joys, Emily arrived. Bouncing with energy and enthusiasm, ready to leap into a new day of fun and activity with her little group of campers. *Oh yay!*

Of course she wanted to know what we were looking so sad about. I wasn't in the mood to go through it all again, so Kenneth repeated the story I had just told him.

Emily looked grim and shook her head, like I knew she would. Just like a teacher or a parent would. And then came the lecture. 'Well, Brett, you only have yourself to blame. If you hadn't been out there, none of this would have happened.'

'Yes, Mum,' I mumbled sarcastically.

'What's Mr McArthur doing about it?' Kenneth asked.

I shook my head sourly. 'He really hooked into me this morning and told me I should be ashamed of myself for hurting "poor Mr Watson". He said if there were any more incidents, he would call my parents.'

'Well, do you blame him?' Emily asked in her know-it-all way. 'You're always causing problems at school. Why should he think this was any different?'

I shrugged my shoulders. She had a point, but I wasn't going to admit it.

Emily continued. 'If you had stayed in your cabin, you wouldn't be in trouble now. It's all your own fault, you know.'

'But there's something funny going on down at the cove,' I spat back at her. 'And Watty is involved in it. Aren't you in the least bit interested in finding out what's going on?'

'No I'm not. And I think this is all just a big dream of yours. Another one of your stupid plans to have fun at someone else's expense. I think you should grow up, Brett. Grow up and get a real life instead of being so silly all the time.'

I couldn't think of anything to say. Emily was just so annoying!

Instead, Kenneth mumbled something.

'What did you say?' Emily asked.

Kenneth spoke up. 'I said, I think Brett is right.'

I don't know who was more taken aback, Emily or me.

'You do?' Emily asked, surprised that Kenneth would say something so radical.

'*You do?*' I echoed, absolutely stunned that Kenneth would agree with me. Especially after all the horrible things I had done to him.

'Yes, I do. Because . . . because of what happened last night,' Kenneth responded.

'I can't see that what happened between Watty and Brett proves anything,' Emily answered in that snooty voice of hers.

'That's not what I mean,' Kenneth replied. 'It's what happened before that. *Before* they had their fight.'

By now I was becoming frustrated with Kenneth's

waffling. 'Come on, Kenneth, spit it out. What are you babbling about?'

'Well, I followed you to the edge of the bush last night. Then I got . . . well, I was frightened. I didn't want to go in. So I stopped and watched you from there. That was when I saw them.'

'Saw who?' I asked, totally confused.

'Watty and the other man. *The huge one!* He was much bigger than Watty. They were waiting in the bush near the water's edge. I only noticed because one of them dropped something and I heard the noise. You were too far away by then, and I couldn't get your attention.'

'Who was the other man?' Emily asked doubtfully. She really didn't sound convinced by Kenneth's story.

I must admit I did wonder whether it was just his imagination at work, and that he was simply trying to get back in my good books after running away.

Kenneth shrugged his shoulders. 'I don't know. It was too dark to see clearly. They must have heard Brett walking through the bush, because all of a sudden they stopped what they were doing and ducked down. When Watty started sneaking through the trees towards Brett, the other guy started walking back along the beach. Towards me. *He was huge!* Honest. If he'd found me I'm sure he would have killed me. That's why I ran away.'

I snorted grumpily. His story sounded reasonable, but I was still too unhappy to let him off the hook completely. I was also more interested in the mystery man who had been with Watty. If Kenneth was telling the truth, there was *definitely* something funny going on down at the cove.

Emily, however, was not convinced. 'I still think you're making something out of nothing. Both of you. After all, Watty is the caretaker. There could be any number of reasons why he was out there.'

'In the middle of the night?' I questioned sarcastically. 'Yeah, right! Even you aren't *that* stupid, Emily.'

Emily went bright red. At last I'd managed to rattle her. 'No, I'm not stupid, Brett Rigby. It's just that . . . well . . . it's none of your business what Watty does. Why can't you be normal and stay out of things that don't concern you.'

I laughed out loud. '*Be normal* . . . huh! If that means being like you, forget it. I couldn't think of anything more boring.'

'Suit yourself,' Emily snapped angrily, 'but there's no way I'm getting involved in your silly games.'

And with that cheerful comment, she turned and stalked off to her cabin.

Chapter 13

The rest of the day turned into a living nightmare. We spent the whole time doing team-building activities on the field. *The whole day!* Stuck with Kenneth who had left me to be strangled, and Emily who wanted me to be 'normal'.

I haven't a clue how, but we managed to get through the day and complete all the activities without killing each other. I was seriously threatened at one stage. But not by Kenneth or Emily.

It was late in the afternoon and I needed a drink. I wasn't all that thirsty, but it was a chance to get away from the other two, even if only for a few minutes. Mr McArthur saw me strolling back to the dining room and bellowed at me to hurry up. He gave me two minutes to get back to the field.

The last thing I needed was more trouble with Macca, so I started running. Across the field, round the corner of the dining room and smack into someone coming the other way. The other person was much bigger, and I had the wind knocked out of me. Gasping for breath I looked up.

It was Watty!

He had a nasty grin on his face and a big bandage on

his arm. He moved closer to me, forcing me back against the wall.

'Well, well, well! If it isn't my favourite camper.'

I didn't say anything. I was still winded from the collision *and* I was frightened.

'Nothing to say for yourself? That's surprising for someone with a very big mouth.'

The grin dropped from his face to be replaced by an evil sneer. 'Well, I've got a few things to say, so listen carefully, sonny.'

Watty came so close, I could smell garlic on his breath. I turned my face away from the stink but he reached up, grabbed my face in one grubby paw and made me look him in the eye. He squeezed so tight, my teeth hurt and my eyes watered.

'I warned you nicely to stay out of things that didn't concern you, but you wouldn't listen. I meant to hurt you last night and the next time you cross my path I'll do more than hurt you. Understand?'

Watty squeezed so hard, I was sure my teeth would break. I blinked through the tears and nodded. He let my face go. My heart was pounding and I was shaking all over. I wanted to rub my aching jaw, but I was too scared to move. It was all I could do to stop myself from bursting into tears.

Watty lifted his hand again and I flinched, sure he was going to hit me. But he just patted me gently on the head. 'That's a good boy,' he murmured softly. 'I'm so glad we understand each other.'

Then he turned and walked away.

I stood there trying to stop shaking and then managed to stumble to the toilets. Grabbing the soap, I scrubbed my face to get rid of the dirt from Watty's sweaty hand. Still too shaky to run, I walked slowly back to the field. Mr McArthur yelled at me for taking so long, but I didn't care. After what had just happened with Watty, Macca didn't scare me in the least.

By the time I crawled into bed that night, I was totally wiped out. The camp I had spent months looking forward to had turned into a total disaster.

Surely it couldn't get any worse!

Chapter 14

It was midnight, and pitch-black. Thick, dark clouds completely covered the moon. A cabin door opened slowly and a small figure slipped out, gently shutting the door so as not to disturb anyone.

The figure stood back against the side of the cabin in the shadows and watched. And waited. At last, confident it was safe, it moved out of the shadows onto the path. The security light on the corner of the cabin shone brightly down on her. On Emily Burton.

She was just about to step off the path to move away from the cabin, when she caught a glimpse of movement across the grassy slope. Movement coming up from the cove.

Two shapes were walking up from the water, standing close together and whispering. They were both adults. One was short, the other much bigger.

Emily quickly stepped back into the shadows of the cabin doorway. Heart thumping, she prayed she would not be seen. If she were caught out at night, her mother would never forgive her!

As the two figures rounded the far end of the cabin block, the lighting on that corner spotlighted them. Emily's eyes widened.

The smaller figure was Watty. The other shape — the bigger one — she didn't recognise. *But he was massive!* It must have been the man Kenneth had seen. He had been telling the truth! The two men disappeared around the corner of the block.

Emily waited in the shadows, breathing deeply, wondering what to do. Should she stay or follow?

She made up her mind. Stepping out of the shadows, she ran lightly to the end of the block and stopped. Carefully, she looked around the corner. Nothing!

She moved quickly to the next corner and peered around carefully, just in time to see the giant of a man walking back towards her. He must have heard her running along the path!

Emily spun back against the wall, shaking. Looking from right to left, she searched frantically for somewhere to hide. There was nothing. In a few seconds, he would find her.

As quietly as she could, Emily ran back the way she had come. Surely he would hear the noise of her feet on the concrete! Turning the last corner, Emily paused.

Nothing . . . still nowhere to hide. And her cabin was too far away. The giant would catch her before she could get there. Without thinking, she opened the nearest cabin door, stepped inside and quietly pulled the door shut behind her.

Where could she hide? It was too dark to see if any of the bunks were empty. And there were no cupboards in the cabins.

Her mind racing, she dropped to the floor and squeezed underneath the bunk closest to the door. She lay there on the cold concrete, trying to catch her breath and listened.

And waited. And sniffed. *Ohhhh, what was that revolting smell?*

Something underneath her head absolutely reeked. Lifting her head, she pulled out the object and tried to make out what it was.

Socks! Filthy, wet, disgusting, smelly socks. And then she realised where she was. *In one of the boys' cabins!*

She closed her eyes tightly and screwed up her face. Oh no, if she were caught in the boys' cabins, her life was over. *She would never live it down!*

That thought disappeared as she heard the door squeak. And open. Very, very slowly. Turning her head, she could make out two enormous feet stepping softly into the cabin. They stopped centimetres from where she lay under the bunk. Emily stopped breathing. And waited. Waited to be discovered. Surely he would find her!

The feet didn't move. What on earth was he doing?

Her chest was starting to ache. Her eyes started to water. She had to breathe soon. But he would hear her. She was sure of it! So she bit her lip, closed her eyes and waited. And waited.

And then she heard the feet move, ever so quietly, and the door shut. Opening her eyes she looked to where the feet had been. *Nothing!* He had gone.

As quietly as she could, Emily breathed out and sucked in great gulps of air. Her heart was beating rapidly, and her mind was racing.

That had been close. Too close! She couldn't risk getting caught again.

Slipping out from under the bunk, she tiptoed through the darkness to the far side of the cabin. Carefully avoiding the shape huddled in the sleeping bag, she stepped up onto the end of the bunk nearest the wall, pulled back the corner of the curtain and looked out the cabin window. Just in time to see the two men walk across the grassed area and around the corner of the Recreation Hall.

No way was she following them over there!

Still shaking, Emily quietly slipped out of the cabin and returned to her own room. To her bed.

To safety.

Chapter 15

While I did get more sleep that night, I didn't feel any better when I woke in the morning. Not surprising, considering what I had to look forward to. Just another day trailing around behind Emily and Kenneth.

And just when I thought things couldn't get any worse . . . they did!

We were sitting eating breakfast. I was at the same table as the rest of my cabin, but I wasn't saying anything. The mood I was in, I didn't feel much like talking to Danny or the other guys.

The door to the dining room banged open and in stormed Macca, along with one of the parent helpers. Macca looked *totally steamed*.

He stomped to the front of the room, his face black with anger. Five rows of tables went dead quiet, just like that. For a minute he stood there and said nothing. Breathing heavily, he looked us up and down.

The whole class, from one table to the next. Started with me . . . *and* finished with me. I had no idea what was coming, but I knew it couldn't be good.

Macca started talking quietly. So quietly, I could hardly hear him. 'I have been taking school camps away for seven years now. I have thoroughly enjoyed *every* camp I have been on . . . until *this* one.'

His voice became louder. 'Parts of this camp have been good. Other parts,' he stared at me as he said this, 'I have not enjoyed in the least. The parts I have not enjoyed have been the nights.'

Macca was now yelling. 'The nights when *every single individual* on this camp should have been asleep in his or her cabin.' Macca was now glaring at me angrily. The whole class might have been there, but he was talking to me alone.

'Last night,' Macca continued in a sarcastic voice, 'someone broke into the school equipment trailer. *Someone* decided to borrow some of our gear.'

He started walking slowly down the dining hall towards our table. *Towards me!* I couldn't take my eyes off him. 'Someone broke the lock on the trailer and removed all our climbing rope and the marker buoys we use for kayaking. Now, we can't go climbing and we can't go kayaking.'

A low groan rumbled around the room. Macca stopped at our table. Right beside me. Everyone knew he was talking to me. From the corner of my eye, I could see kids staring at me. They weren't happy faces.

I didn't blame them. I was angry as well. Kayaking and rock climbing were the two best activities at camp. And now we couldn't do them!

I felt like standing and screaming, '*Stop looking at me. I didn't do it!*' But I didn't. I sat there without saying a word, while Macca continued.

'These two activities were to be the focus of today's programme. Obviously, we are not doing them. At least, not yet. Not until the rope and the buoys are returned. I cannot imagine why *anyone* would take them. I can only imagine this is some foolish prank carried out by someone eager for attention.'

Macca turned and glared pointedly at me. 'Well, whoever took them certainly has our attention. Wouldn't you agree, Rigby?'

I tried to speak, but nothing came out. I just nodded my head instead. I felt ill, sick to my stomach.

Macca finally turned away and started walking slowly back to the front of the hall. 'You will now go and tidy your cabins and then meet in your small groups to fill in your camp diaries. While you are in your groups, you might like to have a talk about this unfortunate incident. If anyone knows anything . . . *anything at all* that might help us solve this problem, I suggest you come and see me.'

Mr McArthur looked us up and down one more time, starting and finishing with me *again*, and then stormed out of the dining room.

Chapter 16

We sat at one of the picnic tables outside the dining room: Kenneth, Emily and I. Our diaries lay in front of us, but no one was writing anything. Nobody said anything. Neither of them would even look at me.

Kenneth just stared into space like he does. Emily fiddled with a hair tie.

I broke the awful silence. I couldn't stand it any more. 'I'm dead meat. For once I've done absolutely nothing wrong. Macca thinks I took this stuff. Everyone thinks I took this stuff. *You think I took it!*'

Kenneth turned to me and snorted. I had never seen him so angry. 'Do you blame us, Brett? You're the one who always does this sort of thing. You're the practical joker. No one else is stupid enough to do something like this. Why don't you own up and get it over and done with? Why should we have to suffer because of your dumb ideas? Sometimes the things you do are funny, Brett, but not this time.'

'OK, OK, I can see why Macca and you guys think I took the stuff. And you're right. I admit that sometimes I go overboard with the jokes. But that's all just for fun. This is different. Can't you see that? I mean . . . what am I going to do with a pile of rope and some buoys? I didn't do it,' I wailed. '*Honest, I didn't do it!*'

Disgusted and obviously not believing a word I'd said, Kenneth just shook his head and turned away from me.

Desperate for someone to believe me, I turned to Emily. She continued fiddling with her hair tie and wouldn't look up at me. Clearly she didn't believe me either.

For once, Emily, never short of a word, didn't have *any* to waste on me. Her silence was almost worse than all the lectures she had ever given me. At least then she had been talking to me!

I let my head drop into my arms on the table and moaned quietly to myself, 'I'm history . . . I'm history . . . I am *totally* history.'

'Maybe not,' a quiet voice said. I lifted my head. Emily was looking at me, her face pale, her eyes tired. There was something else in her eyes I had never seen before. Almost like . . . uncertainty.

Yes, that was it! Normally, Emily was so sure of herself. But not now. 'What did you say?' I whispered, now not even sure I had heard her correctly.

Emily sighed. 'I said, maybe you're not history.'

Kenneth turned around and looked at Emily, just as much confusion on his face as on mine. 'What are you talking about? Of course Brett's history. Macca is going to have a field day with him.'

'You're right, Kenneth. *If* he did it. I don't think he did.'

'You don't?' I burst out. I was staggered not only that someone actually believed me, but even more by the fact that the 'someone' was Emily. She was the last person I imagined would take my side.

'Why not?' Kenneth asked, just as surprised as me.

'Because . . .' Emily sighed, struggling to find the words. 'Because . . . I think someone else did it. And I think I know who it was.'

I could hardly contain myself.

One minute I was dead meat; sure I was going to have to face the hangman for something I hadn't even done. Now, a tiny ray of hope was beckoning. 'Come on,' I pleaded impatiently. 'Who did it? Who was it?'

Emily continued uncertainly, almost sadly. 'One of them was Watty. I don't know who the other one was. It might have been the man Kenneth saw down by the cove the other night.'

There was silence for a moment as her words sank in and then Kenneth asked the obvious question. 'But how do you know?'

Emily shifted uncomfortably on the seat. 'Because . . .'

'Yes?' I encouraged. I had absolutely no idea what she was going to say.

And then her words came in a flood, as if it was a relief to get them out. 'Because . . . last night I went out, after everyone was asleep, to have a look for myself. I had to know for sure! And I wanted to prove you wrong, Brett, after you called me stupid and all that, but it looks like you were right after all and . . .'

Emily's voice trailed off weakly, embarrassed that she had been wrong about me.

I didn't say anything, not even 'I told you so'. Instead, I gaped at her, totally astonished by her words. And then I roared with laughter. Little Miss Proper Emily, who never does anything wrong, sneaking around camp in the middle of the night! Maybe there was hope for her after all.

Kenneth's jaw dropped. He was just as surprised as me that Emily would do something so daring. But all he said was 'wow'. And then even louder, 'WOW.'

Emily went as red as a tomato. 'I really don't see what's so funny, Brett Rigby. And you can stop your "wowing" right now, Kenneth Thompson.'

'Hey, it's cool,' I replied, throwing my hands up defensively. 'I'm not laughing *at* you. I just think it's amazing that you would do something so . . . well . . . so *bad!* What if you'd been caught?'

'Well, I wasn't. Unlike you, Brett Rigby, I'm too careful to be caught.' Now Emily was sounding more like her normal snobby self.

'So what did you see?' I asked eagerly. 'Did you see them breaking into the equipment trailer?'

Emily shook her head. 'No, not exactly. But I did see them walking in that direction. It was after midnight. I was coming out of my cabin when I saw them walking up from the cove. I'm sure they didn't see me.'

'Wow,' said Kenneth again, even more impressed than before. His eyes were as big as dinner plates. It struck me then that maybe Kenneth liked Emily . . . a lot!

Giving Kenneth a filthy look for this latest admiring comment, Emily continued.

'They went over the grassed area towards the Recreation Hall. That's when I lost them. I didn't dare follow them across there. It's too open, with nowhere to hide.'

'So how does that prove they broke into the trailer?' Kenneth asked doubtfully. 'If you didn't see them . . .'

Realising what Emily was getting at, I interrupted. 'The trailer is stored around the corner of the Rec Hall, right where they were heading. *It must have been them.*'

Emily nodded thoughtfully. 'That's the way I see it. When Mr McArthur did his rave at breakfast, I realised what they must have been doing. And I think that's why Watty spun his ghost stories when we met him the first time down by the shed. You know, the stuff about keeping safe in our cabins at night? I think he just wanted to make sure we stayed out of the way so he could get up to mischief.'

Excited, I leapt up. 'Yes! That's it. It all fits. Now all we have to do is go to Macca and tell him what you saw. Then I'm off the hook.'

'Ah, not so fast, genius,' Kenneth interrupted. 'For a start, while Mr McArthur is more likely to believe Emily than you, how is she going to explain being out at that time of the night? Macca is not going to be impressed with that. And then, there's the small matter of proof. Emily didn't actually *see* them break into the trailer. And look how easily Watty covered his butt last time you accused him. No, you're going to need more than this before you go to Macca.'

Glumly, I slumped back down on the seat, my hopes crashing down around me. Kenneth was right. Macca would think it was another scheme I had come up with to get out of trouble.

Proof! I needed to get proof that Watty was up to no good.

But how was I going to get it?

Chapter 17

Emily, Kenneth and I talked about the missing gear and what Watty and his buddy might be doing with it.

We had no idea. We couldn't imagine why they would need the rope and the marker buoys.

Kenneth got all excited and suggested they might be searching for treasure in the cove, using the buoy to mark the spot and the rope to raise the treasure.

I scoffed at that idea and told him the story of the treasure was a load of old nonsense. Most likely they'd stolen the gear so they could sell it.

Whatever they were doing, I needed proof. I had to catch Watty and the other guy up to no good. Or even better, catch them with the missing gear. If I could do one of those two things, Mr McArthur *had* to listen to me.

I also knew I'd have to go out at night again to find the proof. The thought made me feel sick, but I knew there was no other time to do it. There were too many adults around in daylight for me to go snooping around camp. And Watty was too smart to do anything during the day.

No, much as the thought frightened me, I'd have to

go out at night. And it had to be *tonight*. I couldn't afford to wait, as there were only two more nights before we left for home. I was running out of time . . . fast!

Emily and Kenneth offered to come with me, but I said no. If something went wrong or I was discovered, I didn't want them involved. I was in so much trouble it wouldn't really matter for me. Apart from this, I wasn't really sure it would be a good idea to take them. Kenneth had run away once. He might do it again, just when I needed him. And while Emily was beginning to surprise me, I wasn't at all certain she was ready for really dirty work.

That night, I didn't have to wait long to sneak out of the cabin. The guys were going to sleep really quickly now. Everyone was tired from all the activities we were doing during the day. Because of this, the 'guards' weren't on duty as long.

Outside the cabin, I waited in the shadows to make sure no one was about. It had been a scorcher of a day, and the sky was still cloudless. A full moon made it easy for me to see some distance. It would also make it easy for anyone else to see me. I had to be careful.

When I was sure it was all clear, I crept along in the shelter of the cabins until I was able to slip into the bush on the edge of the clearing. I stayed just inside the bush-line all the way down to the cove. Every so often I stopped, looked around and listened. Nothing!

At the edge of the cove I crouched just inside the bush and waited. From my spot I could see down towards

Watty's shed and back up towards the camp. I waited. *And waited*. I didn't have my watch with me so I had to guess the time. I think about an hour must have passed when I first noticed it.

Not on the beach or in the bush where I had been looking for action, but out on the water!

The long wait had made me stiff and sore. I stood carefully to stretch the muscles in my legs and looked out across the flat water of the cove. That was when I saw the light.

At least . . . I thought it was a light. It might have been moonlight reflecting off something shiny. But there shouldn't have been *anything* shiny on the water. And certainly not in the middle of the night! My eyes ached as I peered out across the water. It was faint and flickering but *definitely* there.

I crouched back down for a while and tried to work it out. I had expected any action to take place on the beach or near the shed. Or maybe around the camp. But definitely not on the water. How was I going to check it out?

I looked to my right and had my answer. The boat shed!

Crouching low, I scuttled across the sand to the shed. Praying it would not be locked, I tried the door.

It opened.

Pushing the door back to let some moonlight inside, I stared around. Racks of kayaks stretched across the shed. In one corner, more racks held life jackets and paddles.

Trying not to make too much noise, I slid one of the boats out of its rack and carried it down to the water's edge. Running back, I grabbed a paddle and a life jacket.

I pulled on the jacket and then, lifting the paddle, I raced back down to the water's edge. My heart was pounding in my chest, and not just from running.

I crouched by the kayak and looked out over the water. Though the moon was nearly full, the night was still dark. The water was black and I couldn't see anything beneath the surface.

For a moment, my imagination went nuts and a surge of panic gripped me. I wanted to drop the paddle and run back to the safety of my cabin. But I didn't. *I couldn't!* I had to find out what was happening.

Taking deep breaths to calm my shaky nerves, I pushed the kayak into the shallow water and hopped in.

Lifting the paddle, I started stroking slowly out into deeper water. I could see the light flickering ahead of me and kept moving towards it. The only sound was my breathing and the slap of the paddle in the water. Looking over the side of the boat, all I could see was blackness. Cold, unfriendly . . . nothingness.

The water trickling off the blades of the paddle onto my hands was icy. It added to the chill I was feeling inside. My lips were dry and cracking. I tried licking them with my tongue, but my mouth was dry as well.

About halfway to the light, I stopped paddling and just sat. There was no sound now. Nothing. I looked all around. Nothing! No sound . . . no movement. I was alone. Completely alone in the middle of an icy cold, frightening cove in the middle of the night.

Once again the panic nearly swept me away. Angrily shaking it off, I started paddling again, faster now towards the light. It might only have taken another five minutes and I was there.

And that's when I got my first surprise. It wasn't a light. It was a bright red buoy.

Chapter 18

A shiny metal plate was screwed onto the side of the buoy. It was the moonlight reflecting off the plate that I had seen from the shore. Taking a penlight out of my pocket, I switched it on and examined the plate. Engraved on the plate were four words — *Property of Allenvale School*.

I let one end of the paddle go and punched the air. Yes! I had found the proof I needed.

Paddling closer, I pulled up alongside the buoy. Reaching out, I carefully lifted the dripping buoy from the water. Attached to the ring on the bottom of it was a rope. Nylon climbing rope! Success again! I couldn't believe my luck.

And then, my luck ran out. *Completely.*

With a violent jerk, the buoy was pulled out of my hands and into the water. It gave me such a fright, I nearly fell in after it. The kayak tipped crazily from side to side as I struggled to keep my balance. Frantic to stay in the boat, I dropped the paddle in the water.

My mind raced, desperately trying to understand what had just happened. The buoy hadn't slipped out of my hands; something had pulled it from my grasp. *Something . . . under the water.*

Breathing deeply and holding tightly to both sides of the kayak, I frantically twisted my head from side to side, trying to see anything in the water. It was hopeless. The water was as black as oil and I couldn't see a thing.

The paddle! I had to find my paddle. Without it, I would be stuck out in the middle of the cove, with *something* down there.

Desperately looking around, I spotted it on the other side of the buoy. Scooping my hands in the water, I managed to move the kayak and catch up with my paddle. Gratefully picking it up, I started to turn around the buoy to head back to shore.

Without warning, the buoy bobbed violently in the water, and a stream of bubbles broke the surface beside it. Horrified, I froze and stared at the bubbles until they had all disappeared and the buoy had stopped rocking.

Once again I could feel my heart racing in my chest. My hands were wet on the paddle — from picking it up out of the water or from sweat, I couldn't tell.

I had to get out of there.

Slowly, so as not to disturb whatever was down there, I started dipping the paddle in the water and moving towards the shore. It had taken me at least ten minutes to paddle out to the buoy, and the shore now seemed an awfully long way from where I was sitting.

I paddled quietly for a few minutes and nothing happened. I looked back at the buoy and it just sat there not moving. No more bubbles rising from the depths. I started to relax and began paddling a little faster now, keen to get off the water.

About halfway to the beach, I stopped and looked back again. To my horror, the moonlight revealed a stream of silver bubbles making a line from the buoy to my boat. A direct line! The bubbles finished about twenty metres from where I was sitting.

Totally panicked, I dug the paddle into the water and started stroking as fast as I could towards shore. The kayak rocked and swayed as I threw the paddle at the water, slapping first one side and then the other. I didn't care how rough my paddling was, as long as I kept moving. Fast!

Fifty metres from the shore, my arms ached and the muscles in my shoulders burned from the pain. But I didn't slow down. I kept thrashing the water, pushing the kayak along as fast as I could.

I took a quick look over my shoulder and what I saw almost made me cry out in terror. Less than ten metres behind me, a slick, wet, black fin appeared out of the water in a swirl of bubbles. Just like a shark fin!

Moaning now, I turned away from the creature and paddled like crazy towards the shore. So close now . . . yet still so far with this monster behind me. Forty metres . . . thirty metres . . . closer and closer. Still it hadn't caught me. Twenty metres to go and I knew, I knew I would make it.

I took one last look over my shoulder to see where the monster was. That look saved my life. I'm sure of it!

As I turned, I caught a glimpse of a shining, black tentacle swinging through the air. A tentacle with curving claws that glinted in the moonlight. I ducked without even thinking and felt a rush of wind past the back of my head. A sharp, stinging pain burned down my back and then the kayak rocked violently backwards as the claws dug into the end of the boat, somewhere behind me.

Sobbing with pain and fear, I dug the paddle into the water and splashed like a maniac through the last few metres of water to the beach. I didn't even wait for the kayak to run up on the beach. Dropping the paddle, I pushed myself up out of the seat and despite the kayak rocking wildly, I managed to fling myself over the front and onto the sand.

I landed roughly, bruising my hands and knees on the pebbles littering the beach. I didn't care. I was on dry land and off the water.

My whole body ached. All over. My lungs, my arms, my back . . . *everything* hurt. But still I didn't stop. I was too close to the water . . . to *whatever* was in the water.

Gasping for air, I pushed myself off my knees and scrambled up the beach, not stopping until I reached the bottom of the grassy slope. Only then did I stop and look back at the cove. The moonlight reflected off a huge, bulging eye rising out of the water. It glared at me with absolute hatred. Then, hissing and spitting, the creature's slimy head sank beneath the surface of the water in a swirl of angry foam and bubbles.

Chapter 19

I didn't even make it to breakfast the next morning before Macca caught up with me. And you know who dobbed me in?

Watty. Who else?

Macca dragged me out of my cabin and down to the beach. Watty was standing there beside the kayak I had used the previous night. I had been so frightened after escaping the beast, I hadn't even thought about putting it away. Smart, huh?

Macca glared at me angrily. 'Mr Watson came to me this morning. Apparently someone decided to do a bit of midnight kayaking last night. Know anything about it, Rigby?'

I stood there, shuffling my feet in the sand, trying to figure out what to say. In the end, I told the truth. 'Yes sir. It was me.'

Macca shook his head in disbelief. 'Do you have *any* idea how foolish that was, Rigby? Kayaking in the middle of the night by yourself! Do you know how dangerous that was?'

I certainly did. It had been a whole lot more dangerous than even Macca could have imagined. I didn't say that, however. I just stood there. So did Watty, with that permanently nasty grin all over his face.

Mr McArthur continued. 'What on earth did you do it for? Why did you go out? You could have fallen out and drowned with no one there to help you.'

I shrugged my shoulders. There was no point telling him anything. From where we were standing, I could see out onto the water. There was no sign of the buoy. It was long gone. Along with the rope. And Macca was never going to believe me. I had found the evidence . . . and lost it again.

I stood there, silent. My head down, feeling totally miserable. I felt sick to my stomach. And the grazes on my back ached from the creature's claws.

Watty spoke up. 'Not only was he reckless going out alone, he's also damaged the boat. Look at that.'

He pointed to the back of the kayak. Just behind the seat were four deep gashes on the top of the boat. I hadn't seen them last night. The sight of them now brought my stomach up into my mouth. I had been so lucky!

Not that Macca was feeling sorry for me. 'Well, that's the last straw, Rigby. You've gone too far. Though I can't prove it, I suspect you are responsible for the missing equipment. Now we have reckless behaviour and damaging camp property. I warned you yesterday what would happen. I'm calling your parents and they can come and pick you up. Your camp is finished!'

Once more I said nothing. I stood there looking at the ground. There was no point. Macca wouldn't believe me. While I didn't like it one little bit, I actually didn't blame him. Emily was right. All my practical joking had finally caught up with me.

And Watty had done a perfect job of fooling him. Watty had been too clever for me. He was turning Macca against me, and there was absolutely nothing I could do about it.

Chapter 20

As it turned out, Macca was only half right. I didn't end up going home. Not that day anyway. Dad was out of town on business and Mum's car was away being fixed. I would stay at camp for one more day until Dad returned from his trip.

Mr McArthur was not pleased.

Still, camp might as well have been over as far as I was concerned. I had to follow Macca around *all day!* He didn't trust me at all and wouldn't let me out of his sight. And any time he did have to go off somewhere, one of the senior kids was left guarding me. Boy, they sure made the most of it. Talk about bossy! I couldn't even breathe without asking permission.

But if that was bad, there was worse to come. That night, I was going to have to sleep in the cabin with Macca and the parents. *How gross was that?* Bunked down with a bunch of boring, snoring adults!

The only good part of the day was sitting at lunch with Kenneth and Emily. Wow, who'd have thought at the start of camp that I would look forward to spending time with those two? Incredible!

No one else would sit with me or even talk to me. All the other guys in the cabin gave up on me after the gear went missing. Even Danny. Some friends!

As we ate lunch, I told Kenneth and Emily what had happened the previous night. At first they didn't believe me when I told them about the creature attacking me. That changed when I gave them a quick look at the deep scratches on my back.

His face pale, and his eyes wide in horror, Kenneth quizzed me. 'What do you think it was?'

I shook my head, feeling sick again at the thought of the creature. 'I have no idea what it was. But I don't think it was a ghost. It was too real for that.' I shivered, feeling the pain in my back again. 'No, it wasn't a ghost. Whatever it was, it was certainly protecting something in the cove. Whatever that buoy was marking last night.'

Emily frowned, tucking her hair back behind a bright yellow headband. 'I think you're right. I don't think it's a ghost at all. I think Watty spins his ghost stories to keep people away from the cove. But what is he up to?'

I shrugged unhappily, feeling totally sorry for myself. 'Doesn't matter now anyway. I had my chance and I blew it. I lost the only proof I had.'

Emily shook her head. 'I think you're wrong. I don't think you had anything.'

Puzzled, I looked up. 'What do you mean?'

'Even if you had managed to bring the buoy and the rope back, you wouldn't have been able to prove anything. Watty was nowhere around. You wouldn't have been able to prove he had taken them.'

Kenneth nodded thoughtfully. 'Yes, Emily's right. It

wouldn't have proven anything. You needed to find Watty *with* the buoy and the rope.'

Emily sat up suddenly, her eyes sparkling, her hands waving excitedly. 'Yes . . . yes, you're right. Oh, Kenneth, you're brilliant!'

Kenneth actually blushed. 'I . . . I am?'

Emily nodded her head enthusiastically. 'Yes. *We have to find Watty with the gear*. That's it.'

I shook my head, totally confused. 'Hold on, I'm lost. What are you getting at?'

Emily looked at me patiently like I was a little kid. 'The buoy and the rope are not out on the water now, are they?'

I shook my head, still not seeing what she was getting at.

Emily sighed as if she was dealing with a complete idiot. 'So they must be hidden somewhere. Right?'

I nodded, still confused.

But Kenneth wasn't confused. 'The shed! They must be in the caretaker's shed. The shed he didn't want *anyone* snooping around.'

Emily nodded her head. 'Right, Kenneth. The very same shed that you and I are going to break into this afternoon.'

Kenneth went as white as a sheet!

Chapter 21

Even though he had been horrified when Emily suggested they break into the shed, it was Kenneth himself who came up with the plan. From being super scared he became super spy.

He was so excited. The way he figured it, if they planned it right, they wouldn't even have to break into the shed. *Watty would let them in.*

Late that afternoon, Kenneth and Emily saw Watty walking down to his shed, ready to pack up for the day. Trying to look as relaxed as possible, they strolled down to the cove a few minutes after Watty.

From where they were standing on the beach, they could see Watty unlock the shed and walk inside. Perfect timing.

Kenneth looked worriedly at Emily. 'Are you sure you want to do this?'

Emily nodded nervously. 'Yes. Well, no. I don't want to do it, but we don't have a choice. Not if we want to help Brett.'

Kenneth took a deep breath. 'OK. Let's do it then. I'll give you a few minutes to get into position.'

Emily disappeared quickly into the bush. A few minutes later, Kenneth followed. As quietly as he could,

Kenneth crept through the bush until he was around the back of Watty's shed. He crouched and waited. Then, hoping Emily was ready, he took three large stones out of his pocket and stood. Taking aim, he chucked the first stone high into the air towards the shed. *It missed!*

Kenneth groaned quietly, wishing he had practised his ball skills in P.E. Taking the second stone, he tried again.

Yes! Success this time, as the stone crashed down on the roof. He heard Watty swear angrily inside the shed. He must have gotten a fright when the stone landed. Kenneth hurled the last stone as hard as he could towards the shed. Success again! It smashed onto the tin roof.

Kenneth ducked down and waited nervously. He couldn't see the front of the shed, but the swearing became louder, so Watty must have come outside. Then he heard Watty yell. '*Hey you!* What do you think you're doing? Come here, you little brat.'

From where he was crouching, Kenneth saw Watty run past the end of the shed and into the bush. *Yes! It was working*.

Emily had shown herself when Watty stepped out of the shed, just like they had planned. She had run off and was drawing Watty away from the shed. Now it was up to Kenneth.

He scampered through the trees and around the corner of the shed. Pausing, he looked down the path Watty had taken. There was no sign of him. Good.

Kenneth slipped into the shed and looked around. He had to find the gear. And quickly!

Watty was too smart to leave the rope and buoys lying around in the open. They must be hidden. Kenneth looked under the workbench. Nothing there. In the corner lay a plastic groundsheet. He lifted it. Nothing under there.

He shoved all sorts of stuff around roughly. Time was running out. Watty would be back soon. He dug under a pile of sacks in the corner and took the lids off some wooden crates. Nothing. Nothing at all!

Kenneth looked frantically once more around the shed and then stopped, breathing heavily. There was nowhere else to look, nothing else to search.

There was no rope and no buoys. The missing gear simply wasn't there.

Chapter 22

That afternoon seemed to take forever to pass. I followed Macca around the whole time like a lost sheep, wondering what Kenneth and Emily were doing.

Boy had they changed. Both of them. Miss Goody-Two-Shoes was taking risks, and for once, the Alien was actually doing something useful. Or maybe they had always been like that, but I had never noticed.

Anyway, when Macca finally let me go to dinner, I actually ran all the way to the dining room. I couldn't wait to see how they had got on. I stopped dead in my tracks when I walked through the door.

Stopped dead by the sight of Kenneth — white-faced, tears in his eyes, horribly upset. And Emily was nowhere to be seen.

'*Where is she?*' I burst out, before Kenneth could say anything.

'I . . . I . . . don't know,' he sobbed. 'Something's gone . . . gone wrong. I just know it.'

We were getting funny looks from the kids sitting at the tables, so I took Kenneth by the arm and pushed him out the door. I led him around the back of the dining hall where it was quiet.

Kenneth was still sobbing, his breath coming in big

gasps. Embarrassed, I patted him on the shoulder, trying to calm him down. 'It's OK, Kenneth. Settle down and take it quietly.'

He took deep breaths and told me what had happened, right up to when he went into the shed.

'There was nothing there! No buoys, no rope, just tools and things. My great plan didn't work.' He started sobbing again. 'And now . . . now Emily's gone as well.'

Kenneth was beside himself. I felt really sorry for him. Reaching out, I patted him on the shoulder again. 'So, where did you and Emily arrange to meet? You know, after it was all over.'

Kenneth wiped his eyes with one grubby hand. 'We . . . we said we'd meet at the back of the Recreation Hall, by the equipment trailer. I went straight there after I got out of the shed. I was only in the shed for about two minutes. Just long enough to see the stuff wasn't there. Then I went straight to the Rec Hall and waited. She didn't turn up. Something bad has happened, I know it!'

I thought for a minute and then said hopefully, 'Maybe she's been held up? Maybe she had to hide out for a while? She's not dumb. She can look after herself.'

Kenneth shook his head miserably. 'I don't think so.'

'Why not?' I asked, puzzled as to how he could be so certain.

'Because I went looking for her. I waited for ages, but when she didn't turn up, I went to find her. I searched all over that section of bush and all around the shed. I didn't find her, but . . .'

'But what?' I asked nervously.

'I didn't find Emily, but I did find this.'

Kenneth showed me something he was clutching in his hand. I hadn't even noticed it all the time we had been talking. It was a bright yellow headband.

Emily's headband. And it was stained with dark spots. Spots of blood!

Kenneth looked at me and I looked at him. For ages, neither of us said anything. We just stared at the head-band . . . and the spots of blood.

All sorts of horrible thoughts went through my mind. We were in it up to our eyeballs. Emily was in trouble big time, and needed help. But we couldn't go and see Mr McArthur. He simply wouldn't believe us. And there was no one else we could get to help. We were miles from anywhere. With a sigh, I lifted my head and groaned.

Macca was coming towards us.

I was surprised he'd left me alone for so long. I turned quickly to Kenneth. 'Listen. You've got to think of some-thing. Some way we can find Emily. And . . . and some way to distract Macca so I can get out of his clutches.'

Kenneth spluttered, 'But I can't. You're the one who comes up with the crazy plans, not *me!*'

I shook my head. 'Not like this. It takes me ages to come up with schemes and we don't have time. You're the one with the brains — use them and do it fast. You have to. *We've got to find Emily!*'

'But I can't. Look what happened to my last great

plan. That's why Emily's in trouble in the first place.'

Macca was nearly on top of us. I moved closer to Kenneth so Macca wouldn't hear. '*Just do it*,' I hissed. 'Get me away from Macca and work out how we can find Emily. *Now!*'

Mr McArthur fixed me with an evil look and took Kenneth gently by the arm. 'Is Rigby bothering you, Kenneth?'

Kenneth looked at me, then Macca and then back to me. His mouth opened and shut several times, but no sound came out. Finally he looked at Macca and said in a quiet voice, 'No, sir. He's not bothering me. It's just a misunderstanding. He . . . he wanted me to help him with something. But . . . I can't.'

Macca looked at me sternly. 'Got the message, Rigby? Whatever it is you want, and I'm sure it can't be good, Kenneth isn't going to help. Now, stop bugging him! Is that clear?'

Kenneth stood beside Mr McArthur, staring at his shoes. He wouldn't even look at me. I couldn't believe it. Kenneth had dumped me in it. Just when I needed help — *when Emily needed help* — he'd run away again.

I sighed heavily. It was hopeless. I was going to have to save Emily myself.

Macca glared at me. 'I said, *is that clear*, Rigby?'

I nodded, feeling totally sick as I did. 'Yes sir, it's *all* very clear.'

Then, without looking at Kenneth, I turned and walked away.

Chapter 23

Night fell and I was stuck in the cabin with a parent helper watching me. Macca was determined I wasn't going to spoil his last night in camp. He was off in the Rec Hall with the other adults, organising evening activities for the class.

The parent 'guarding' me wasn't happy. He clearly didn't want this job and wouldn't even talk to me.

For ages I lay on a bunk trying to think of ways to help Emily. All I came up with was a massive headache. I couldn't even work out how to get out of the cabin.

Occasionally, another parent would come into the cabin to get something. Listening to the adults talking, it was clear no one had even missed Emily.

And from the noise coming out of the Rec Hall, evening activities were obviously still going strong. In all that noise, bodies running in all directions, no one would notice she wasn't there. Emily wouldn't be missed until bedtime, and that was hours away. By then, it could be too late to start searching for her.

For the hundredth time I groaned and rolled over, desperately trying to get my dull brain working. But it was hopeless! There was too much pressure and too little time.

For the hundredth time I also cursed Kenneth for being a useless coward. I would have given *anything* to have his brain at that moment. Yes, for once, I actually envied Kenneth. I wanted to be like him. Anything to help Emily. Boy, how things can change in a few short days.

And just as I was thinking this, all the lights went out. In the cabin *and* outside. No lights . . . nothing! Total darkness.

For a moment, there was complete silence. Then I heard the kids in the Rec Hall all start laughing and yelling at the same time.

'Hey, what's going on?'

'Who turned the lights out?'

'Aaagh, get off, you're standing on me, you fat lump!'

And all sorts of other silly comments. Then it went deathly silent again. For a very, very brief moment. Until the whole camp exploded into a riot of bangs, noises and terrified screams.

The parent guarding me didn't even say a word. Muttering under his breath, he scrambled anxiously around in the darkness trying to find a torch. Eventually he found one, then without saying a word to me, he was out the door to see what was happening.

For a second I just stood there. I think I was partly in shock, wondering what was happening outside. The screams and yells were still going on, and I could hear my classmates panicking and running in all directions. Through all that noise I could make out adult voices calling, but I couldn't work out what they were saying.

Then my brain started working again. *I was free!*

My guard had found his torch on a table against the wall of the cabin. Stumbling through the darkness, I crossed the cabin and banged into the table. Running my hands over it, I found what I was looking for. Another torch. *Yes!*

I flicked it on to see if it worked. It did. Switching it off, I ran to the door and looked out. Nothing. It was still pitch-black. I couldn't see anything, but then again, nobody could see me. Perfect! I was out the door and gone without another thought.

Running around the corner of the cabin, I headed straight for the slope leading down to the cove. A few shapes ran past me — kids yelling and screaming — and one banged into me. I grabbed the body and shook whoever it was.

'What's happening? What's going on?' I demanded.

From the voice, I could tell it was one of the girls and that was all. She was babbling so much I couldn't tell who it was.

'It's a ghost . . . one . . . one of the pirates. In the hall, up on the stage. He fired . . . fired a gun at us. *Ohhhh, I want to go hoooome!!!*'

And then she pushed me away and was gone.

I stood there in the darkness trying to understand what she had said. Ghosts? In the Rec Hall? Firing guns?

I couldn't make any sense of it, so I just shook my head and started running again down the slope. I was nearly at the bottom near the beach, when something burst out of the trees to my left.

The moonlight broke through the clouds, and I could see whatever it was quite clearly. A horrible figure. *An awful shape.* It glowed. It shimmered. And it seemed to float above the ground.

I heard a quiet moan start up and then realised it was coming from me. I couldn't move. The shape must have heard the moan, because it turned to face me.

It was clearer now. I could see it was dressed in rags, all torn and tattered. On its head was a crumpled three-cornered hat. Over one eye was a black patch and tucked into a wide black belt was a pistol. The figure raised a ragged arm holding a ghostly, shimmering cutlass. Then it pulled the pistol from its belt and cackled horribly. An awful, ghostly laugh, hundreds of years old!

Chapter 24

Scared witless, I dropped to my knees, whimpering. 'Don't shoot me. Please, please don't shoot me!'

The ghost threw back its head and laughed even harder. There would be no mercy here.

Shivering, I sobbed quietly to myself. *This was it!* This time I was a goner . . . for sure! Why didn't I stay in the cabin where it was safe? I couldn't stop shaking, I was so scared, waiting for that ghostly gun to fire. Waiting to feel the awful pain of the shot. I closed my eyes and prayed that it wouldn't hurt too much. But still the shot didn't come.

Instead, the pirate ghost just kept on laughing. It laughed so hard, in fact, that it started coughing and choking and spluttering.

Confused, I lifted my head and stared at the ghost. It was still standing there, shimmering in the dark, but the gun was no longer pointing at me. The ghost had dropped it on the ground.

The shape was standing there, hands on its knees. Trying to get its breath back, and choking from all the laughing. And then it raised its head and in between splutters, spoke to me in a voice that was *definitely* not two hundred years old. '*Got you!* Oh yes . . . got you a beauty. That was so worth all the horrible things you've ever done to me.'

Kenneth?

It was Kenneth! I stared at him, my mouth wide open. A flood of questions bombarded my brain all at the same time. 'What . . . how did . . . what have you?' It was my turn to splutter, kneeling there on the ground like a complete idiot. I was still shaking, my head was spinning and I couldn't even get one decent question out.

Kenneth finally stopped coughing, picked up the gun and grabbed me by the arm. 'Come on, we have to get out of here. Especially with me dressed like this.'

We stumbled down the last part of the slope and into the trees near Watty's shed. Kenneth dropped the cutlass and took off the hat, the eye patch and the strips of ghostly, shining rags that covered his clothes. He stuffed them under a bush. From under the same bush he pulled a small pack he'd obviously hidden there earlier. He opened it and pushed the gun inside. He looked up at me. I could see his white teeth grinning at me through the darkness. 'You never know, we might need the gun later. It worked quite well on you.'

My thoughts still a confused whirl, I finally managed to get half a question out. 'You mean, you did all this just to . . .'

Kenneth finished the question. 'Just to pull a practical joke on you?' He shook his head. 'Sometimes you really are slow, Brett. No, I did all this to spring you from that cabin. To cause a fuss so you could escape.

That's what you wanted, wasn't it?'

I nodded, still trying to get my thoughts together.

He grinned broadly again. 'No, having you on your knees trying not to wet yourself . . . that was just a bonus. I wasn't expecting that. But you can be sure I'll let everyone know about it later. Oh no, I'm not going to forget that one.'

I could feel my face going bright red. I felt like kicking Kenneth, but I was too relieved to be out of the cabin. Instead, I pointed at the glowing rags under the bush. 'What's all that? How did you cause all that fuss? And why did you change your mind?'

Kenneth shrugged his shoulders awkwardly and looked all embarrassed. 'I don't know. I couldn't leave Emily, I guess. Couldn't stand the thought of her out there. Had to do something . . . As for the ghost stunt, that was easy. Everyone's been talking about ghosts and pirates all week; I just built on that. I made up a costume from bits and pieces I found backstage in the Rec Hall. The gun is a starter's pistol from the sports gear. The cutlass is just cardboard covered in tinfoil. I sprayed on some fluorescent paint I found in the art supplies cupboard and the rest was easy.'

He continued, 'The main power board is around the back of the Rec Hall so I waited until everyone was inside, flipped the main switch so all the lights went off and made my grand entrance through the side door onto the stage. When everyone started spinning out, I hoped you would make your escape. I figured you'd head down here, so I came to meet you. Simple really.'

I shook my head in admiration. *Simple!* It was an act of true genius. I punched him playfully on the shoulder. 'It was great, Kenneth, just brilliant. I could never have come up with that one. You're in a class of your own.'

He looked at me with a silly grin on his face. Bet he never imagined I would ever compliment him like that. Mind you, I never thought I would either.

Then I remembered Emily. 'What are we going to do now? We've got to help Emily and I haven't a clue where to start. How are we going to find her?'

Kenneth grinned at me again. 'Don't you worry about that. It's all taken care of. Follow me.'

He stepped out of the bushes onto the beach. Before he could go any further, I grabbed him by the arm and yanked him back into the bushes. He looked at me as if I'd gone nuts. 'What did you do that for?' he asked.

I didn't answer. *Couldn't answer!* Just pointed to the water in front of us. To the trail of bubbles heading straight towards the shore.

Straight to where we were hiding!

Chapter 25

Kenneth didn't have a clue what was coming, so he just crouched there, silent. Having already had one narrow escape from the beast, I started trembling. The grazes on my back started to ache again.

The bubbles, reflected in the pale moonlight, came right to the edge of the water. Then the creature slowly appeared. Its monstrous black head broke the surface first. That horrible, single eye searched slowly one way, then the next. Small, snake-like tentacles came out of its mouth, curving around over its bulky shoulders. The creature's back was a bulging, curving shape, dripping slimy water and weed.

It was huge!

My mouth went dry, and I started to shake. I couldn't help it. Then one large, wet, black tentacle, a huge claw on the end, slipped out of the water and pulled the creature forward onto the sand. The same claw that had scarred my back!

Another tentacle appeared and dragged the beast further up the beach. It moved closer to where we lay. A cold sweat breaking out all over me, I started moaning quietly and pushed myself up from where I was lying. *We had to get away from there.* It would find us and kill us. Nothing was more certain.

Kenneth grabbed me and pulled me back down. Still shaken by his ghost act, and scared witless by the appearance of the creature, I felt ill, too weak to resist. And then I nearly lost it completely.

For the creature opened its mouth wide, its jaw and tentacles dropping down onto the beach, and started gasping air. The rasping sound it made was awful! Not only did it live in water, it could survive on land. It would come after us and kill us . . . *we were dead meat!*

I started moaning louder, but Kenneth slapped one hand across my mouth to muffle the noise. With his other hand he held me down, stopping me from running away. Was he completely mad?

Not twenty metres away, a beast that had already tried to kill me once was lurking in the darkness. *And Kenneth wanted to watch?*

I could hear the creature snuffling, sniffing the air, breathing deeply. Surely it would smell us and hunt us down. Rip us apart with its horrible claw.

That gross, dripping head, jaw dragging in the sand, just searched up and down the beach. Then it stared right past where we lay, up towards the camp. I was sure it would see us, but it just lay there, sniffing and searching.

At last, it rose up in the darkness and crouched for a moment on the edge of the beach. Then, pulling itself free from the water, it finally stood tall. The creature stood on two legs. Two very human-looking legs.

Confused now, I stared through terrified, tear-filled eyes. I blinked to try and see more clearly.

No monster. No beast or creature. *Definitely* no ghost from the depths of the ocean.

It was a man!

Dressed in a black rubber wetsuit, full face mask and diving gear. On his back were twin air tanks with hoses coming around to the mouthpiece hanging loosely on his chest. In his right hand he held a grappling hook with a rope attached to the end of it. The sharp prongs of the hook glinted wickedly in the moonlight.

The man turned and once more looked both ways along the beach. Finally confident no one was watching, he dropped the hook onto the sand. Then he removed the face mask and stripped off the hood of his wetsuit.

He ran his fingers through slick, wet, black hair and then looked past us, up towards the camp buildings once more. The moonlight highlighted his face clearly. There was no mistaking that crooked nose. *It was Watty!*

A rush of hot anger surged through me, and I was all for leaping up and going for him. Kenneth still had his hand over my mouth and felt me move. He tightened his grip, holding me down once more. Breathing deeply, I tried to calm down. Kenneth was right. I had to keep cool. I couldn't take Watty on.

Not like this.

Finally satisfied it was all clear, Watty picked up his hook, mask and hood and started walking along the beach. He disappeared into the bush near his shed.

We waited silently for long minutes until we were sure he was gone and wasn't going to come back. At last, Kenneth spoke quietly. 'Well, the mystery of the creature from the cove is solved.'

I snorted angrily. 'Yes. You knew it wasn't really a ghost, didn't you?'

'Yes. I never did believe in ghosts. I just like spinning stories about them to wind people up. People like you.'

I laughed quietly. 'And you succeeded.'

Kenneth grinned. 'I know. Cool huh!'

I nodded, and then an awful thought struck me. 'The other night, Watty attacked me out on the water. If he'd do that to me, Emily is in real danger. We've got to find her. *Now!*'

Kenneth picked up his pack. 'Right, we'd better get moving then. I think I know where Watty is going. If I'm right, it's the same place he's keeping Emily.'

Without explaining how he knew all this, Kenneth simply turned and walked off into the darkness.

Chapter 26

I followed Kenneth for ages along a narrow path winding through the trees. He was moving quite quickly, so I got the feeling he had been there before.

I didn't have a clue where we were going. The moon was barely bright enough to guide us, but Kenneth seemed to know what he was doing, so I just followed. I had to trust him.

After about ten minutes of fast walking, Kenneth stopped suddenly. I was about to ask what was wrong, when he raised his finger to his lips to silence me. He ducked down and crept forward. Nervously I followed.

We were at the edge of a clearing in the bush. Just ahead of us, the moonlight revealed a small footbridge crossing what looked like a gully or a stream.

On the other side of the footbridge, the bush had been cleared, making way for a small cottage. The outside light was on, making it easy to see across the whole clearing, right to where we were hiding. Beside the cottage, a dented, banged-up jeep was parked. I could make out a dirt road leading away from the cottage.

Kenneth leaned towards me and whispered. 'I figured it out this evening. We were so dumb not to think of it before. Watty *had* to live somewhere. He didn't sleep in his shed or at the camp, so he had to have a house somewhere. I saw him back at camp with Macca just before dinner tonight. When he left, I followed him. Here! I snuck around the back and looked through the windows. There are only two rooms. That's the living area straight ahead coming off the deck. There's just one bedroom off that. That's where Emily is. *I saw her!* Sitting on a chair, all tied up, but I couldn't get to her. Not with those guys there. The only way to the bedroom is through the living area. That's why I came back for you. *We have to do this together!*'

Eyes wide, I stared at Kenneth. *Was he nuts?* How were we supposed to break Emily out of her prison? With two adults guarding her, one of them a giant!

Before I could say anything, someone stepped out onto the deck in front of the cottage. The outside light shone brightly on him. It had to be Watty's buddy, the one I hadn't seen yet.

Like the others had said, *he was enormous!* He must have been at least two metres tall. His head was as big as a basketball. With all his hair shaved off, it even *looked* like a basketball. And he was built like a wrestler. His arms were as thick as tree branches and seemed to hang almost to his knees. I groaned quietly. How on earth did Kenneth think we were going to deal with him?

The man turned and called back through the open door in a gruff voice, 'I'll be twenty minutes. I'll pick up all we need and then we'll decide what to do with that brat.'

The giant shut the door behind him, stomped down

the steps and strode to the jeep. He barely managed to fit in the driver's seat he was so big. The jeep roared into life and wheels spinning, he was gone down the dirt road.

I crouched there, frozen. Couldn't move . . . couldn't think. The giant's words echoed in my ears. '*We'll decide what to do with that brat!*'

Kenneth punched me gleefully on the shoulder. 'Yes! That's one down. Now all we have to do is deal with Watty.'

I stared at him, eyes wide. He was mad. Stark raving bonkers! The odds were certainly easier with the giant gone, but that still left us with Watty. And only twenty minutes before his friend returned. I shook my head, despairing. 'Kenneth! What are we going to do? We don't have much time.'

Kenneth continued staring at the cottage as if he hadn't heard me. I was just about to thump him to get his attention, when he finally spoke. 'Right. Hmm . . . let's see . . .'

He looked at the footbridge, back at the cottage and then back to the bridge again. He scratched his chin thoughtfully. 'Yes . . . yes, it might work. I mean, it's worked once.' He chuckled quietly. 'Yes, especially if he knows it's you. I'm *sure* it will work!'

All of a sudden I felt very, very uncomfortable. 'What might work? And what do you mean, "especially if he knows it's me?" I don't think I like the sound of this.'

Kenneth grabbed me by the arm and pulled me to my

feet. 'No time to explain. Just do what I say.' He bent down and picked up a rock, and shoved it into my hands. 'Here, take this. Now, get across the bridge as fast as you can, run up to the cottage and chuck that through the front window.'

I stared at Kenneth, my eyes wide open in horror. This was his great plan?

He ignored the horrified look on my face and continued, 'When Watty comes out, yell and scream at him. Say whatever you want. Just make sure you get him *really* angry. Angry enough to chase you.'

'And what do I do then?' I asked, convinced Kenneth had finally gone completely insane.

Kenneth shook his head in frustration. 'Run, you fool. What else? *Run!* Back over the bridge to here. Just make sure Watty is right behind you, that's all.'

'And what then? I just wait here for him to come and beat me to a pulp?'

Kenneth grinned. 'Just trust me. You make sure Watty comes back over that bridge and I'll take care of him. Now get moving. We don't have much time!'

Chapter 27

Head spinning, I walked towards the footbridge. I held the rock nervously in one sweaty hand.

Some weapon . . . *some plan!* Boy, if I ever got out of this alive, Kenneth would pay.

Just before I stepped onto the bridge, I had to duck under a low branch hanging across the path. Then I was on the bridge, over it and standing in the small clearing in front of the cottage. I stood there, staring at the large, front window, rolling the rock in my hands. This was madness!

From somewhere behind me, I could hear a worried voice hiss, '*Hurry up*. Throw it, Brett. *Now!*'

Taking a deep breath, I raised the rock and hurled it as hard as I could at the front window.

The window immediately shattered into a thousand pieces. *The noise was incredible!* Even though I knew it was coming, I still stepped back in surprise at the sound of the glass smashing.

From inside the cottage, there was a thump and a bang, the sound of someone cursing loudly, and the next minute the front door burst open. Watty stood there, still dressed in his wetsuit. He glared at me from the doorway.

I took another step back, thinking about how he had

hurt me previously. Then, remembering Kenneth's instructions, I opened my mouth and tried to speak.

Nothing came out!

Watty, however, wasn't stuck for words. He bellowed at me angrily from the doorway. '*What the hell do you think you're doing?* You're nothing but a damned nuisance, kid. I should have scared you off for good the other night!'

That was all I needed to get me going. All of a sudden, I found my tongue. 'You . . . you couldn't scare me. Not . . . not a disgusting, scabby weed like you, Watty. You're so useless you couldn't even scare a cockroach.'

With a furious growl, Watty leapt off the deck. *He didn't even use the steps!* And then he was after me.

Moaning, I turned and ran like I never had before. I just ran and never looked back. I could hear Watty's feet pounding the hard ground behind me. Then I was on the bridge, feet rattling the wooden planks as I tore across.

Almost immediately, the bridge shook violently. Watty!

He was right behind me!

'*Kenneeeth,*' I wailed as I raced off the other end of the bridge. At the last minute, I remembered the low branch, and ducked. My mind barely had time to register that the branch wasn't there, and I was off the bridge and pounding dirt again.

And then there was a loud whoosh and I felt a wave of air brush past the back of my neck.

It made my hair stand on end!

It was followed immediately by a solid clunk and a horrible groan. I didn't have a clue what was happening, but I sure wasn't stopping to find out. I tore through the trees, branches whipping my face in the darkness.

Then I heard Kenneth's voice screaming from behind me.

'*Brett, stop! I got him. Stooooppp!*'

Gasping for breath, I stopped and leaned against a tree. I was shaking so badly, I would have fallen over if the tree hadn't been there. I looked back through the gloom. I could just make out Kenneth near the footbridge. He was jumping up and down like a madman, waving his arms and yelling at me to come back.

I could make out Watty lying in a heap on the ground at Kenneth's feet.

Not moving!

I stumbled back towards the bridge, still shaking badly. Kenneth kept bouncing up and down yelling over and over again. 'It worked. It worked! My plan worked. I did it. I got him.'

Confused, I looked at Kenneth, at Watty on the ground with a huge lump on his head, and then up at the branch hanging once again over the end of the bridge.

Just above Watty's head.

And then it all clicked. Kenneth had pulled the branch back like a catapult, waited for me to run past, then launched the branch straight at Watty. I looked down at Watty. He wasn't moving or making a sound. Kenneth had knocked him out. *Totally!*

Hands on my knees, still gasping for air, I shook my head in disbelief.

This had been his great plan?

'Kenneth,' I panted, 'what . . . what if you'd missed him? What if you'd been too early or too late letting go of the branch? Do you know how lucky you were to get him?'

Kenneth got serious all of a sudden. He scratched his head and thought about it and then shrugged his shoulders. 'I guess so. But it worked, didn't it?'

I shook my head. He was totally missing the point. 'What if you hadn't knocked him out? What . . . what would you have done then?'

Kenneth shrugged his shoulders again. 'I don't know. I hadn't really thought of that.'

I just stood there, shaking my head. I couldn't believe how lucky he had been. But there was no time to waste on this now. Taking a deep breath, I straightened up. 'Right, let's get Emily. *Fast!*'

Chapter 28

Kenneth waited by the bridge, keeping an eye on Watty while I raced to the cottage, up the steps and into the living area.

Kenneth had said the bedroom was off to the right. There was only one door on that wall, so I rushed over and nervously pushed it open.

Relief washed over me when I saw Emily turn anxiously towards me. She was tied to a chair, with a rag knotted across her mouth to stop her calling out. She looked awfully pale and there were tear stains on her cheeks. Above her right eye was a jagged cut, crusted with dried blood.

But she was alive!

Crossing to the chair, I pulled the rag off her face and started tugging at the ropes tying her to the chair. A stream of words poured out of her mouth. 'Oh Brett, get me out of here. *Quick.* Help me. Where's Watty? That awful man . . . the big one . . . he's going to hurt me. I know he is. *Help me, Brett*!'

I tugged at the ropes and tried to calm her. 'It's OK. It's all right. I'll get you out of here. Just sit still so I can get these ropes off.'

Emily continued sobbing. 'Where's Watty? What's

happened? Who else is here?'

The knots wouldn't move! I pushed and pulled as hard as I could, but it was no good. The knots were too tight.

I could feel Emily squirming in the chair, panicking, trying to get free. 'Get them off, Brett. Untie me. *What are you doing?*'

I stood and raced back into the living area. I heard Emily scream after me.

'Brett! Where are you going? Don't leave me here. *Please don't leave me!*'

I yanked open drawers in the small kitchen, anxiously searching for a knife. Anything to cut the ropes.

'Brett . . . what are you doing? Come back here now! *Please?*'

I was doing my best, but Emily's yelling was really getting on my nerves. I called back through the doorway. 'I'm trying to find a knife. To cut you loose. I'm not leaving, Emily, but if you don't shut up, I'm going to put that rag back over your mouth.'

I could still hear Emily sobbing, but at least the yelling stopped.

Yes! I found a small, sharp knife buried right at the bottom of the drawer. Sprinting back into the bedroom, I started sawing at the ropes around her wrists.

'How did they catch you?' I asked breathlessly.

'When . . . when I ran away from Watty . . . down by the shed, I thought it was all going to work. Just like Kenneth planned. But . . . but then I ran straight into Nixon, he's the big guy. He was walking through the bush to meet Watty at the shed.'

'What about the cut on your head? Did they do that?'

Emily shook her head. 'No, that was my own stupid fault. I ran into some bushes while I was running away from them. My headband got stuck and held me up. That's how they caught me. I cut my head on the bushes trying to get free.'

One of the ropes gave way. *Yes!*

I started on the next one. Still two strands of rope to go. I kept talking, trying to calm Emily down. 'What are they up to? What are they doing down at the cove?'

Her voice getting a little stronger and calmer, Emily answered. 'Kenneth was right. They *are* searching for treasure. From the ship that sank in the cove. They have to do it in secret, because the cove is in a regional park. And they don't want anyone else getting in on the act. If word got out there was treasure here, the place would be flooded with treasure seekers.'

The second rope parted. Quickly I started on the last one. The big guy would be back any minute. We had to keep moving. 'So have they found anything yet?'

Emily shook her head. 'No, not yet. That's why they want to keep it a secret. They need to keep searching and they don't want anyone to know what they are doing. Oh, hurry up Brett. *Please!*'

Finally!

The last rope dropped away. Emily stood up rubbing her hands. She was wobbly on her feet from being tied up for so long. Taking her by the arm, I helped her across to the bedroom door.

We were out of there.

And then there was a loud roar, the sound of an engine revving and the screech of brakes.

We were too late.

The giant, Nixon, was back!

Chapter 29

Emily started shaking. I stood there, frozen. I couldn't believe it. We had been so close to getting away, and now we were trapped in the cottage.

Trembling, I looked desperately around the room for somewhere to hide. Apart from a bed in one corner and the chair Emily had been sitting on, there was nothing. Not even a wardrobe.

The window.

It was our only chance. Quickly shutting the door to the living area, I grabbed Emily and pulled her across to the window. Lifting the catch, I pushed it open. It needed oiling and squeaked horribly. I could hear heavy feet stamping up the steps to the front door. A gruff voice called out, 'Watty, I'm back.'

Taking Emily's arm, I helped her up onto the windowsill. I hoped the drop to the ground wasn't too far. She was still shaking, and I wasn't much better. I could feel sweat breaking out all over me.

The footsteps stopped in the other room and Nixon called again. '*Watty?* Where are you?'

I hissed in Emily's ear. 'When you get down, run as fast as you can around to the front of the house and go across the bridge. Kenneth is there.'

Then I shoved her out the window. She hit the ground with a thud and grunted. *Surely Nixon would hear that?* The footsteps started again, moving quickly now towards the bedroom door. I heard Nixon's voice, more anxious this time. '*Watty!* What's happening? Are you in there?'

I pulled myself up onto the windowsill and tried to jump down. But I couldn't move.

I was stuck!

Looking down, I saw the pocket of my jeans was caught on the window catch. Panicking, I tried to pull it free, but it wouldn't move. I reached around, but I was balanced awkwardly and couldn't get my hand to my pocket to lift it off.

The bedroom door burst open, crashing back against the wall. Nixon stood there, his huge body filling the whole doorway. He looked at the empty chair, the ropes lying on the floor and then straight at me, stuck in the window.

For a moment, everything froze.

The giant stared at me, confused and trying to work out what had happened; I stared back at him, absolutely petrified. Then Nixon roared with anger and stormed across the room, huge arms reaching out to crush me.

Sobbing in terror, I pushed against the window as hard as I could and jumped out at the same time. I felt the pocket rip and come free. I landed awkwardly on the ground, banging my left knee.

The pain brought tears to my eyes, but I didn't have time to worry about it. Looking back up at the window,

I could see Nixon, a foul look on his face, glaring down at me.

And then he was gone and all I could hear was his footsteps thundering back through the house. *He was coming out to get me*.

I pushed myself up onto my feet and limped as fast as I could around the corner of the house.

It was hopeless!

My knee hurt too much. I couldn't even walk properly. I leaned against the house and stared towards the footbridge. With the help of the outside light, I could make out Emily and Kenneth on the far side of the bridge. Kenneth frantically waved his arms, urging me to hurry.

Then Nixon raged out the front door. He paused at the top of the steps, looking around. I felt totally ill when his eyes settled on me. No way was I going to be able to run away from him.

I pushed myself away from the cottage and started hobbling as fast as I could away from Nixon. And away from the bridge. There was no hope for me, but I might be able to give Emily and Kenneth time to get away. I heard a bellow of pure rage behind me and the sound of heavy feet thumping down the steps.

I didn't look back. I didn't have to. I knew what was coming. Panting, tears streaming down my face, I kept hopping as fast as I could away from this monster of a man.

I didn't get far.

Something blasted into the back of my head, flattening me on the ground. All the breath was knocked out of me and I cracked the side of my face on a dead branch. I went all dizzy and nearly fainted there and then.

Rough hands grabbed me and flipped me over on my back and then pulled me up until I was hanging in midair. Nixon bawled at me, spit spraying my face. 'Where is she, you little rat? The girl! Where's she gone? *And what have you done with Watty?*'

He shook me like I was a rag doll, until my teeth rattled and my head ached. '*Where are they? Tell me dammit!*'

I didn't have a chance to answer. A screaming, wailing tornado ran straight into the back of Nixon. It hit him so hard, he dropped me and fell to his knees. My eyes ached and I kept going dizzy. But I could still make out what the tornado was. It was Emily.

Emily gone totally ape!

Hanging onto Nixon's back, screaming, punching and scratching. She'd gone absolutely berserk.

She had come back to help me.

And she wasn't the only one. Kenneth was running towards me as well.

I tried to push myself up to help Emily, but my head went all fuzzy. I sank back onto my knees and groaned. Shaking my head, I looked up. Emily still had her arms wrapped around Nixon's face and neck, and was clawing at his eyes and nose.

Nixon was roaring with pain and swatting at Emily

with his huge hands, trying to knock her off. One direct hit and she would be a goner.

Kenneth had stopped about ten metres away and was just standing there. Watching! *What on earth was he doing?*

I screamed at him, 'Do something, Kenneth. Help her. *Now!*'

Kenneth, wide-eyed with horror, stared at me, then back to Emily . . . and then turned and ran away. I dropped my head in disbelief. *Noooo!* This couldn't be happening again. Not again.

But it was.

I was too sick to help Emily and Kenneth, the coward, had turned tail and was gone. Sobbing with anger and fear, I dragged myself towards Nixon. In my hand I clutched the dead branch I had banged my face on.

Meanwhile, Nixon had managed to land an awkward blow to the side of Emily's head. Her grip loosened and she slipped off his back and fell to the ground behind him. Helpless! Beside himself with fury at Emily's unexpected and violent attack, Nixon had totally lost the plot. Swearing and cursing, he didn't even bother standing up, just turned around on his knees and reached out with those huge, ugly hands for Emily's throat.

'*Noooooo!*' I screamed at him as loud as I could.

Exhausted, I pushed myself up onto my feet and lifted the branch, ready for one last desperate attempt at saving Emily. And then I froze, still clutching the branch. And Nixon froze, still reaching for Emily's neck, as a commanding voice echoed across the clearing.

'Freeze, sucker! Step back and put your hands up against the wall. Now!'

Chapter 30

I looked across the clearing, expecting to see a policeman standing there. Nixon looked as well, clearly expecting the same.

It wasn't the police, however.

It was Kenneth!

Standing with his feet wide apart, arms straight out in front, both hands holding the starter's gun pointed straight at Nixon's head. I groaned. Kenneth really had been watching too many cop programmes on TV.

As if he had heard me, Kenneth called again. 'I said, step back and put your hands up against the wall. *Move it, scumbag!*'

What wall was he talking about? We were in the middle of the bush, for crying out loud! What on earth did Kenneth think he was doing? Threatening a violent giant of a man with a starter's pistol? *He truly was nuts!*

Fortunately, Nixon seemed to be just as confused as me. Uncertain, he shuffled back on his knees away from Emily and stood up. He was obviously trying to work out what Kenneth was up to.

From this distance, and in the dark, the gun certainly looked real. Nixon clearly wasn't taking any chances on what this crazy kid would do with it. But it couldn't last. It wouldn't take long for him to figure out Kenneth was bluffing.

Gathering my last bit of strength, I stepped forward. I stayed as far away from Nixon as I could and poked him in the back with the sharp end of the branch. Snarling in pain, he turned angrily towards me.

My hand shaking, I pointed back the way we had come. 'Get moving. *Now!* Back to the cottage. Before . . . before he lets you have it.'

He stood there glaring at me, but didn't move.

Kenneth picked up on what I was trying to do. He yelled at Nixon. 'You heard him. Move. *Now!* Or . . . or you'll end up just like your pal Watty.'

That got to Nixon. He might not have been sure how serious Kenneth was, but he did know Watty had disappeared. He had no idea at all what had happened to his partner. Nixon started trudging slowly back towards the cottage.

Breathing deeply, I stumbled along after him, keeping plenty of distance between us. Kenneth used his brain and stayed well away also, but kept the gun aimed at Nixon the whole time. I couldn't even look to see how Emily was. She would have to wait until Nixon was sorted.

And that was the next problem. What were we going to do with him? Just in front of the cottage, I took a deep breath and called out to Nixon. 'Stop there. Lie down on the ground on your stomach with your hands behind you.'

He looked at me as if he was going to refuse, and then stared once more at Kenneth and the gun. Then giving me another filthy look, he finally got down on the ground. I sighed quietly in relief. I don't know what I would have done if he had refused.

Emily hobbled up, rubbing her tear-streaked face where Nixon had hit her. Kenneth moved over beside us, still keeping the pistol pointed at Nixon. 'What do we do now?' I whispered quietly.

'We've got to tie him up,' Emily replied, her voice more than a little shaky. 'We . . . we need some rope.' Silence, as we all thought. Emily was right, but where were we going to find rope?

'Look in the jeep,' Kenneth suggested. 'There must be a tow rope or something in there.'

Stepping up to the back of the jeep, Emily and I looked inside. I lifted a cover and saw the missing marker buoys and the climbing rope. Yes! Finally, we had all the proof we needed, and Watty and his pal caught fair and square with it.

But we needed to get the gear and the two men back to camp.

To Mr McArthur.

I frowned, trying to wrap my brain around the problem. And then, for once in my life, it all came together very quickly.

Chapter 31

I started unhooking one side of the jeep's tailgate. 'Quick, Emily, undo the other side.'

Emily gave me a funny look, but did as I asked. A few seconds later, the tailgate was down and the pile of climbing rope lay on the ground beside the jeep.

I took one end of the rope and quickly made a loop in it. Then I walked over to where Nixon lay on the ground. Taking a deep breath, I dug up my meanest voice. 'Keep your hands together behind your back.' Watching him closely, I spoke to Kenneth in a loud voice. 'If he moves *anything*, shoot him in the leg. OK?'

Kenneth grunted, as if nothing would give him more pleasure.

Then I leaned over, slipped the loop over Nixon's wrists and pulled tight. *Really tight!* Nixon yelped in pain. Good, I thought, payback time!

Keeping the rope tight, I made him stand up, climb into the back of the jeep and lie down. It wasn't easy with his hands tied behind his back, but that was his problem.

When he was in and lying down, I tied more rope around his wrists and then around his legs. I wasn't any good at knots, so I just used plenty of rope, wrapping his hands and legs together as tightly as I could.

When I was satisfied Nixon couldn't move, I left Kenneth to watch him while Emily and I ran to get Watty. I was worried he might have come to, but he was still unconscious. Kenneth had certainly done a good job on him!

It was hard work, but Emily and I dragged him by the legs back to the jeep. It took the three of us to lift him up into the back, but we managed it.

We weren't very gentle with him and he got banged around some more, but that was too bad. Grabbing the rope, we wrapped it around Watty and then tied the two men to each other, to the jeep, pretty much to anything we could find.

And we only just finished it in time as Watty started stirring. At first he was confused, but when he realised what was happening, he started spitting curses at us. Even though he was tied up, it was still pretty scary. We put the cover over the two of them so we didn't have to look at them.

Then we walked away from the jeep and collapsed on the steps of the cottage.

I started thinking about everything that had happened and began to shake. Then I threw up all over the ground. I spat and coughed until the vomit was all out of my mouth.

Tears in my eyes, I looked at the other two, feeling embarrassed at chucking up everywhere. I needn't have worried.

Emily was crying her eyes out and shaking just as much as me.

Kenneth was sitting there like a zombie. Silent, staring at nothing. But I knew what was going through his head. We had been so lucky. So very, very lucky.

We could never expect to be that lucky again.

Chapter 32

I was exhausted and ached all over, but I knew we needed to get moving. I looked at the other two. They looked as bad as I felt. We needed to get back to camp. To get help. Kenneth especially did not look very good.

'Right,' I said quietly, 'time to go.'

Kenneth looked up and asked in a tired, little boy voice, 'But how do we get them back to camp?'

I didn't feel much like smiling, but I lifted my head and managed a weak grin. 'Simple.' I pointed at the jeep. 'We drive.'

That really got them going. I knew it would. It took their minds off the horrible experience we had just survived.

Emily gaped at me. '*We do?* And who, may I ask, is going to do the driving?'

I couldn't believe how good it was to hear that smarmy schoolteacher voice again.

Pointing to my chest, I replied, 'Why me, of course. Any complaints?'

Kenneth looked a bit doubtful. 'Ah Brett, do you *know* how to drive?'

I put on my best 'hurt' look. 'Of course I do. I watch

my dad when he drives. And I play *Gran Turismo* all the time on the PlayStation. I mean to say, how hard can it be?' I don't know why, but they just didn't seem convinced.

Still, we all crammed in the front of the jeep. It was only designed for two people, so it was a bit of a squeeze. That made changing gears even harder. And it was a pretty old jeep, so it wasn't running very smoothly.

At least those were my excuses.

I don't think it was all my fault that I stalled seven times. And the accelerator must have been stuck, because it kept bunny hopping. And it really wasn't my fault about the sign. You know, the one at the main gate to camp saying *Welcome to Pirate's Cove*. They really did put it a bit too close to the entrance.

Driving through the main gate, I couldn't resist pushing the pedal to the floor and sliding around the corner. I mean, how was I to know the sign was so close? Surely they'd be able to fix it up. When they find all the bits, that is.

I did't even think Mr McArthur would be too worried about that. No, for once, Macca wasn't going to be angry. Not with Brett Rigby driving right up to his front door in a jeep. And *not* when he saw what we had in the back.

Boy, was Macca in for a surprise!

Chapter 33

The silence hanging over Pirate's Cove was almost complete. The only disturbance was the sound of a noisy vehicle hiccupping through the night. The water in the cove was still. Nothing moved, apart from the occasional ripple caused by the soft evening breeze.

Without warning, a stream of bubbles rose to the surface near the edge of the cove. From the middle of the bubbles, a large, dark object suddenly popped out of the water and bobbed up and down. The breeze slowly pushed it towards the shore.

The object, a piece of wood blackened with age, floated up onto the beach. The rotting wood was full of holes after many, many years under the water.

As dawn broke and the sun rose, letters carved into the wood long ago could just be made out.

The letters formed one single word.

REVENGE.